COWBOY OUTLAW

LORI WILDE &
KRISTIN ECKHARDT

D1564117

"Don't say I didn't warn you."

Cade Holden looked up from the sheet of plywood he was measuring and scowled at his little brother.

Only Trace wasn't so little anymore. He'd just turned twenty-six, and at six two, stood just an inch shorter than Cade. They'd spent most of the morning repairing horse stalls on Elk Creek Ranch and the sun shone brightly in the big, blue Texas sky.

"Warn me? You've been predicting catastrophes ever since Grandma Hattie started Cowboy Confidential. Don't you think you might be just a little paranoid?"

Trace Holden snorted. "It's not just a temporary staffing agency and you know it. She's been determined from the start to see each one of her six grandsons roped and saddled with a wife. Now she's four-for-four in that matchmaking scheme she calls Cowboy Confidential." He shook his head. "Well, I'm not sticking around to be victim number six."

"Number six? Who's victim number five?"

"Just take a look in the mirror, pal," Trace placed his hammer on a sawhorse. "You are bride bait, and Grandma Hattie is all set to reel one in for you."

Cade shook, then pulled a stubby pencil out of his shirt pocket. It was unseasonably warm for January, and he'd already peeled off his chore jacket and rolled up the sleeves of his flannel shirt.

He began marking off measurements on the wood, refusing to let this ridiculous conversation slow his progress. He'd taken over the Holden family ranch three years ago, shortly after earning his general contractor's license. His carpentry work had paid off, both around the ranch and with jobs he'd picked up in Pine City.

He stuck the pencil back in his shirt pocket, then glanced at his brother. Trace might have a few more pounds on him than Cade, but obviously not as much brain. He was also an inveterate playboy. "Look, Trace, you've got to get over this marriage phobia of yours. It isn't healthy."

"And I suppose your plan to have women audition for a chance to be your wife is what you call healthy?"

"Definitely. I'm planning to marry for keeps. As soon as I find the one who fits all my requirements."

Trace visibly shuddered. "Not me. I'm hightailing it out of here."

"And going where?"

"Colorado. I'm headed to the Denver Stock Show and hauling some of Uncle Pete's purebred Longhorn bulls with me." Trace cleared his throat. "Lauren wants to see me while I'm there."

The name of Trace's ex-fiancée made Cade stop in his tracks. "Lauren? It's been three years since she broke it off with you. I didn't know you two were still in contact."

"We're not. I mean, we haven't spoken since she took that job in Denver. But she sent me a text message a couple of weeks ago asking if I'd be at the stock show and saying she wanted to meet with me."

"And you agreed?" Cade asked, remembering how long it had taken his brother to get over Lauren.

"I sure did, because it's the perfect setup." Trace pulled a bandana handkerchief out of his pocket and wiped the sweat off the back of his neck. "If Grandma Hattie believes Lauren broke my heart again, then she'll give me plenty of time to recover." He gave his brother a rueful smile. "Could take me months or even years before I'd be ready for romance again."

Cade couldn't tell if he was serious. "You'd deceive Grandma Hattie like that?"

"Deceive is a strong word. I don't know how I'll feel when I see Lauren again." Trace looked off in the distance. "Maybe the sparks are still there."

"You're overthinking this, Trace." Cade picked up his power saw and placed it carefully into position on top of the plywood. "I just told Grandma Hattie straight out that I won't be working a job for Cowboy Confidential. Between the ranch and my contractor jobs, I simply don't have the time. Especially now that I'm renovating that old building in the business district for Carly's new café."

Carly Weiss, their future sister-in-law, was a talented chef who intended to open an upscale farm-to-table café in the heart of Pine City.

Trace nodded. "I heard about that. Sorry I won't be around to help you."

"It's no problem." Cade smiled. "I asked Grandma Hattie to find me a carpenter's assistant from Cowboy Confidential. That way, I can support her business and get the help I need."

"Smart," Trace said with an approving nod. "And she agreed?"

"She sure did." Cade removed his brown leather cowboy hat to wipe the perspiration from his brow.

"So, I avoided her matchmaking trap and didn't even have to leave Texas to do it."

"I remember Jack thinking he'd avoided her trap, too." Trace folded his arms across his chest. "And then he proposed to Carly less than a month after meeting her. Grandma Hattie made that happen." Trace leaned toward him and lowered his voice. "Be afraid, Cade. Be very afraid."

"Hey, I like Carly," Cade said in defense of his future sister-in-law. He picked up the power cord to the saw and walked toward the horse barn to plug it in. "And she's good for Jack."

"I like her too," Trace said, following him. "But I'm still not sticking around Pine City."

Cade shook his head. Trace was actually running scared. And for what? Some illogical fear that Grandma Hattie could make him fall in love with a woman against his will?

Cade wasn't about to let that happen to him. He'd be getting married all right, but to a woman of his own choosing. A woman who fit the exact blueprint of the future he wanted to build. And he'd made that clear to his grandmother, in no uncertain terms. She'd taken the news well. He frowned down at the level in his hand. Maybe a little too well. Maybe he should have another talk with her, just in case...

As if she were psychic, Hattie Holden appeared at

that moment, turning her new silver SUV into the long gravel driveway of Elk Creek Ranch and heading straight for them.

"Here comes trouble," Trace said with a grin. Then he ducked into the horse barn and out of sight.

"Hey, get back here," Cade called after him, but to no avail. As his grandmother parked nearby, he noticed she wasn't alone. A man in his early twenties sat in the passenger seat beside her. He'd seen him somewhere before but couldn't quite place him.

"Cade, I've got a surprise for you," Grandma Hattie called out to him as she climbed down from the SUV and walked toward him. She wore a red plaid flannel shirt, blue jeans, and her favorite pair of cowboy boots. Her silver hair was styled in two braids that hung over her shoulders, making her look younger than her seventy-one years.

Cade glanced toward the horse barn, but Trace was nowhere to be found.

"You won't believe it," Grandma Hattie said when she reached him, the young man trailing a few feet behind her. "I've found the perfect carpenter's apprentice for you. Meet Gino Galetti."

The scrawny young man stepped forward, his dark hair pulled into a loose ponytail. "Hello, again." His voice was reedy, and he didn't make eye contact.

But as soon as Cade heard him speak, he remembered where he'd met this guy. He stifled a groan as he reached out to shake Gino's hand. His grandmother had a bad habit of taking in strays. He recalled another stray named Weasel, whom she'd taken under her wing a while back. But even Weasel would make a better carpenter's apprentice than Gino. Anyone would be better than Gino. "Don't you already have a job as a barista?"

"Not anymore." Gino yanked his hand away, then folded his arms across his chest. "I told you he doesn't like me," he said to Grandma Hattie. "Didn't I tell you? I spill one cup of coffee on him, and he holds a grudge forever."

"I'm sure that's not true," Grandma Hattie said, reaching over to pat Gino's arm. "Is it, Cade?"

It was darn close to the truth, Cade thought to himself. That hot coffee Gino had dumped in his lap had come perilously close to doing serious damage. Gino was obviously as dangerous as the rest of the infamous Galetti family. They were notorious in Pine City for their criminal ways.

Cade shuddered to think of the havoc Gino could wreak with a nail gun. "Look, it's nothing personal," he explained. "I just prefer to work with someone who has actual carpentry experience."

"I made a birdhouse in seventh-grade shop class," Gino said, widening his brown puppy eyes.

"And I'm always doing little repairs around the house."

"Hammer something for him," Grandma Hattie suggested, picking up the hammer from the sawhorse and handing it to Gino. "Show him what you can do."

Cade took a cautious step back. "That's really not necess—"

Gino took a swing at one of the braces Cade had just built. Wood splintered as the brace split in two at the impact and fell to the ground.

"—ary," Cade finished, looking in dismay at his shattered handiwork.

"There's more where that came from," Gino said proudly, flipping the hammer high in the air.

"I'm sure there is," Cade said, quickly reaching out to grab the flying hammer before Gino did any more damage. "But I really can't afford you."

"Oh, don't worry, dear," Grandma Hattie chimed, smiling sweetly at her grandson. "Money won't be a problem. Since I'm mentoring him, I'll cover half his wages. He needs a little polishing, but I think he has potential."

Gino stepped forward. "And I just can't take the stress of working at the Armadillo Coffeehouse anymore," Gino explained, his voice quivering. "The menu is so complicated and some of the customers can be so rude. You dribble a little coffee on them, and they start screaming about lawsuits and third-degree burns."

Grandma Hattie wrapped one arm around Gino's narrow shoulders, then looked over at Cade. "The barista life just isn't for him. I thought working with his hands would be soothing and you could use the help."

It might be soothing for Gino, but not for Cade. "Maybe you should take a vacation instead?" he told the guy. "You could lie around on a beach somewhere and soak up the sun."

"Sand gives me a rash." Gino swallowed hard, his Adam's apple bobbing in his neck. "For once in my life, I'd like to be good at something. Just give me a chance."

Grandma Hattie leaned toward her grandson and lowered her voice. "Please, Cade. For me."

Damn. Now she had him. He'd give his right arm for Grandma Hattie if she wanted it. She and his late Grandpa Henry had raised Cade and his five brothers after their parents were killed in a car accident. He'd only been five years old at the time, but his grandparents' unconditional love had filled the horrible void in his life.

She'd always been there when he'd needed her.

That's why Cade would agree to take on Gino as an apprentice. Which might actually cost him his right arm. Not to mention a leg and numerous fingers.

"Anything for you, Grandma Hattie," Cade said, leaning over to kiss her cheek.

Her blue eyes widened. "Anything?"

"Almost anything," he amended before he found himself saddled with a blind date on top of everything else.

"But Cade..."

He held up one hand. "We've already talked about this. Besides, I need to clean up soon. I have a date tonight with Kimberly."

Grandma Hattie wrinkled her nose. "You're still seeing her. She's so..."

"Sweet? Nice? Giving?"

"Exactly. She'll kill you with kindness. Or boredom. Or both. You need a woman who will challenge you. Someone who will add some excitement and unpredictability in your life."

"That's exactly what I don't need," Cade countered. He had his future drawn out as neatly as a set of building schematics. And he knew the exact specifications he required in a wife. He'd even made a checklist to use for rating potential candidates.

Grandma Hattie sighed. "Spoken like a man who hasn't met the right woman yet."

Cade couldn't argue with her. Not because he

agreed, but because Gino had started up the power saw and the noise made it impossible to think, much less speak. He turned to catch sight of the saw flailing wildly in Gino's hands. "Put that thing down before you hurt someone!"

But it was too late.

Chloe Galetti didn't feel at home in prison, despite the fact that several members of her extended family resided at the North Texas Women's Correctional Center. Still, she faithfully made the rounds each visiting day, bearing gifts and Galetti family gossip.

First, she saw Aunt Wanda, serving two-to-five years for petty larceny. Then Cousin Kit, serving ten months for floating bad checks. Her other cousin, Nora, was in again for violating her probation.

And then there was her mother.

"Did you know I'm up for parole soon?" Eileen Galetti asked, flicking a piece of lint off the sleeve of her bright-orange jumpsuit.

"In twenty-one days. That's what I wanted to talk to you about." Chloe cleared her throat, then looked at her mother through the plexiglass partition. She'd rehearsed this speech during the one-hour trip from Pine City, determined to convince Eileen to go straight once and for all. "You'll have a much better chance of making parole if you've got a good job lined up."

"You don't have to worry about me, dear. I know how to take care of myself. Besides, I'm really overqualified for most jobs," Eileen mused. "And I refuse to work in another laundry." She frowned down at her chapped hands. "Just look at what that harsh detergent has done to my cuticles."

Chloe leaned forward in her chair. "Mother, you can't be picky this time. And if you want to stay out of prison, you absolutely cannot work for Uncle Leo again."

"But he lets me set my own hours."

"You were a courier for his money-laundering operation!"

"He had a wonderful dental plan."

"You're going legit this time, Mom." Chloe set her jaw, determined to be as stubborn as her mother. "I mean it. Gino needs you on the outside, and so do I."

Eileen frowned. "What's the matter with Gino? What did he do this time?"

Chloe didn't know where to begin. It seemed her younger brother was always suffering some sort of crisis. "Well, he's still upset about his broken engagement. I knew it was a mistake for you to fix him up with your cellmate."

Eileen threw her hands in the air. "I thought having a girlfriend might give him some self-confidence. He's so shy around women."

"His girlfriend was convicted of attempted murder!" Chloe exclaimed in a hushed voice.

"But Nanette seemed like such a nice girl when she was my roomie. And she's so pretty. By the way, she's not my cellmate anymore. Her conviction got overturned last month on a technicality. I heard she moved to Florida, so she's out of his life if that makes you happy."

"It absolutely does." Chloe breathed a sigh of relief. "Because the last thing we need in this family is another felon. Now, I think you should move back home when you get out of here and I'll help you find a good, legitimate job."

"You can't afford another mouth to feed, honey. Especially when you're struggling to start your interior design business." She glanced around her, eyeing the prison guard across the room, then lowered her voice to a whisper. "You don't have to go it alone, you know. The family can find a way to funnel you some cash under the table."

"I don't want that kind of help," Chloe said firmly. "You know that. I want to earn my success."

Eileen gave her a wistful smile. "Oh, my sweet Chloe. You've always been the black sheep of the

Galetti family, so determined to stay on the right side of the law."

"Well, this black sheep just got her first big job," Chloe announced, trying her best to sound nonchalant about it. "So, money won't be a problem for a while."

Eileen's face lit up. "What! You got a job!"

"Hey, quiet down over there," the prison guard shouted.

Eileen rolled her eyes, then leaned closer to the partition and lowered her voice. "When did this happen?"

"Just yesterday, actually. I went to pick up Gino from the Armadillo Coffeehouse and ran into one of his favorite customers, a woman named Hattie Holden. She treated me to a cup of coffee and the next thing I knew she was offering me a job to decorate her future daughter-in-law's new café." Chloe couldn't stop smiling. "Apparently, she runs some sort of temporary staffing agency and her daughter-in-law hired her to find an interior designer."

"Hattie Holden?" Eileen's brow furrowed. "Wait a minute, I know her. Her staffing agency is called Cowboy Confidential, right?"

"Yes, it is." Chloe blinked in surprise. "She opened the agency a year ago. But you've been stuck in here for the past five years, so how could you possibly know her? Unless..."

"Don't worry, she wasn't locked up here. She was a guest speaker at our vocational careers class a while back." Eileen smiled. "Sweet lady, but tough as nails too. She sure didn't put up with any sass from the loudmouths in the class."

"I do like her," Chloe said. "And I'm excited about this job."

Eileen beamed. "Well, you can thank me for that. Hattie and I chatted a bit after class that day. I told her all about you and Gino, just like any other proud mama. So Hattie knew where to go lookin' for good help." She leaned forward and lowered her voice. "And she told the class that some of her employees even find love on the job. Maybe you'll be one of them."

"I've heard that rumor," Chloe said, shaking her head. "But I don't believe in mixing business with romance."

"My sensible Chloe." Eileen sighed. "I suppose you don't believe in love, either."

"Actually, I do. But I'm taking a break from the dating cesspool. I just want to focus on building my design business."

Eileen clucked her tongue. "You're on the wrong

side of twenty-five, dear. It's time to stop being so picky."

"I'm not picky," Chloe countered. "As long as they pass the FBI background check."

Eileen laughed, but Chloe wasn't joking. Growing up among the Galetti men had taught her exactly what she didn't want in a man. They were all handsome and charming, but too reckless for their own good. They all had criminal records too. Except Gino, whom she'd managed to keep out of trouble. So far, anyway.

To be fair, Chloe's deceased father hadn't had a criminal record, either. But only because the masterful jewel thief had never been caught.

"Once I make parole, maybe I'll apply for a job at Cowboy Confidential myself," Eileen said playfully. "I still have a few marketable skills. And after spending the last five years in here, I could use some romance in my life."

"That's a wonderful idea," Chloe exclaimed, willing to show enthusiasm for anything that would keep her mother out of trouble. And out of prison. "As soon as you're free, we'll go shopping. We'll buy you a whole new wardrobe."

"I need a new hairstyle, too," Eileen said, fingering her faded brown hair. "And maybe a color touch-up."

"We'll make a day of it," she promised. Thanks to Cowboy Confidential, Chloe would have enough money to give her mother a fresh new start. Hattie Holden's job offer couldn't have come at a better time. Hattie hadn't even asked her for any references. All she'd required of Chloe was to sign on the dotted line. And she'd even given her two bottles of her homemade blackberry cordial as an employee appreciation gift.

Later that evening, Cade sat at his dining room table, knowing he had a decision to make. Kimberly sat opposite him, poised and perfect. Her perfection had actually begun to irritate him a little, but that could just be a side effect of his pain medication.

"How was your dessert?" Kimberly asked after taking a sip of her white wine. She was dressed in a pale-blue silk suit and a pristine white blouse buttoned up to the neck. Her soft-green eyes were serene and focused only on him. Her long blond hair fell like a silk curtain over her shoulders. She was... perfect.

"It's fine," he replied, putting down his spoon.

She carefully folded her white linen napkin and

set it on the table beside her plate. "Blancmange is one of my favorites."

Blancmange was a fancy name for vanilla pudding. That was the problem. Everything with Kimberly was just so... vanilla. Cade sat back in his chair, more irritated with himself than with her. She fit all his specifications, so what exactly was his problem?

Kimberly checked off every item on his list for the perfect wife. Even the truth about his outlaw past hadn't scared her off, yet he'd almost fallen asleep over the soup course. Maybe he was just tired. Calving season would start in a few weeks and he'd been rising before dawn to prepare for it. Then there was the incident with Gino. He flexed his right foot, which was propped up on a chair, and winced slightly at the movement.

"Does it hurt?" she asked, staring down at the bulky gauze bandage on his big toe.

"The numbness is starting to wear off," Cade replied, trying to ignore the throbbing ache in his toe.

She shook her head as she set her spoon down and pushed her empty bowl away. "I never realized ranch life could be so dangerous. You're lucky you only needed four stitches."

"Five," he corrected her, shifting his foot slightly. "And I would have needed a lot more than that if I hadn't been wearing my cowboy boots. It ruined one of them, of course, but saved my foot."

She smiled. "Well, you can always buy a new pair of boots."

Her wholesome smile was beginning to set his teeth on edge. Funny how it had never bothered him before. But then, he hadn't considered the possibility of looking at the smile every day across the breakfast table for the next fifty years.

Until now.

"Although, you really should be more careful." She meticulously brushed a few crumbs off the tablecloth and into her hand. "Thank goodness your grandmother was there to call for an ambulance."

"The ambulance wasn't for me; it was for Gino. He had a panic attack after he dropped the saw on my foot, and then he started hyperventilating."

"Oh, dear," she murmured.

But Cade got the feeling she wasn't really listening. Her total attention was now focused on scraping the dried pink wax off the crystal candleholder.

So maybe she wasn't all that exciting. He wasn't looking for that in a wife. He wasn't necessarily looking for love either, he reminded himself, since that had always proved elusive too. Maybe he just wasn't built that way.

Affection, compatibility, and hopefully passion

were all he needed. Not love. At least not the heart-pounding, soul-searing love that had turned his older brothers' lives inside out. He had a plan. That's why he'd built this four-bedroom home on Elk Creek Ranch two years ago, located about half a mile west of Grandma Hattie's house.

Cade wanted order in his life. Stability. A family. He wanted... vanilla. Which meant he must want Kimberly. He'd probably get used to her smile. And the way her nose twitched when she chewed. All married couples had to make some adjustments, didn't they? It was possible she might even find one or two things about him that irritated her.

The wall clock chimed eight times. Just get it over with, Cade told himself, tired of these annoying second thoughts.

"Kimberly," he began.

She looked up from the candleholder. "Yes, Cade?"

The words stuck in his throat. He cleared it, then took a deep breath. "I'd like to talk about our future."

She leaned forward, daintily folding her hands together on the table. "Oh, I'm so glad. I've been wanting to talk about it for a while now, but I didn't know how to bring it up."

That was another thing he'd noticed about

Kimberly. She usually waited for him to take the initiative.

"You go first," he said graciously, wanting time to compose a proper marriage proposal.

She gave him an affectionate smile. "I never realized what I wanted in my life until I met you. I know we only started dating a month ago, but now everything seems so clear." She gazed wistfully into his eyes. "The first time we kissed, I knew for sure."

Cade wished he could say the same. Unfortunately, their first kiss had created more doubts in him than desire. "You did?"

She nodded. "That's when I knew I wanted to spend the rest of my life in a convent."

He blinked. "What?"

"I'm going to become a nun," she said, her voice quivering with happiness.

"A nun?" he choked out.

She dabbed at her watery eyes with her napkin. "I've already applied to begin my novitiate at St. Mary's. I just wanted one last chance to say goodbye, Cade, and to thank you."

Thank him? He frowned down at his sore toe as her words echoed in his head. He'd kissed her and she'd decided to become a nun. Not exactly a glowing endorsement for his sexual prowess.

"A nun," he murmured, still rocked by her announcement.

She smiled. "Are you surprised?"

"You could say that." He looked up at her. "How long have you been thinking about becoming a... nun?"

"Since I was a little girl." She steepled her fingers together and leaned toward him, looking more animated than he'd ever seen her. "But I didn't want to rush into it, so I decided to have one last fling with a bad boy just to be sure."

One last fling?

He'd been ready to propose to this woman, and she considered him a fling. Cade shook his head, wondering where he'd gone wrong. In all the time he'd spent sizing up Kimberly as potential marriage material, it had never occurred to him that she might be doing the same to him. And he'd fallen short.

He shifted in his chair as he realized the full impact of her words. Her fling with him had convinced Kimberly to take a vow of chastity. And what if there were others? Before Kimberly, he'd dated a lot of women, but never for very long. He'd always let them down easy, but maybe they'd been relieved. Maybe St. Mary's had a run of new nun applications.

"Oh, Cade, you seem upset." Sympathy shone in

her green eyes. "Please know that it's not you, it's me."

It's not you, it's me? That was his line! He straightened in his chair and cleared his throat. This had gone far enough.

"No, I understand," he bit out. "I don't think it ever would have worked between us."

"I'm so glad you see that too. It's taken me a while to build up the nerve to tell you. Then when I walked in here tonight and saw this beautiful romantic table laid out. Candles. Flowers." She shivered. "I almost feared the worst."

For an aspiring nun, she really knew how to twist the knife. "Think of it as a farewell dinner," he said at last. "I doubt you'll get this kind of spread at the nunnery."

"That's true." She smiled as she pushed back her chair. "Gluttony is a sin."

He looked up, surprised to see Kimberly standing now and donning her jacket. "You're leaving?"

"We nuns don't like to keep late hours." She headed toward the front door, then paused to blow him a kiss over her shoulder. "I had a wonderful time tonight, Cade. Thank you for making that delicious dinner."

"Thank you for bringing dessert," he said blankly. Then he pushed out his chair.

"No, don't get up," she said, holding one hand in the air. "I can see myself out. Besides, you and your toe need to rest."

He rose to his feet anyway. Grandpa Henry had taught Cade and his brothers the proper way to treat a lady. He could at least open the door and see her out. But Kimberly, probably fearing a goodnight kiss, gave him a quick wave and sailed out the front door before he could even reach her.

A few moments later he heard the loud roar of a car engine and the sound of tires kicking up gravel. Sister Kimberly had a lead foot. He vaguely wondered if nuns got speeding tickets.

He limped slowly back to the dining room and his gaze fell on the soiled plates neatly laid out on the table. Sitting down in his chair, Cade leaned his head back and closed his eyes. He couldn't wash dishes in his condition. Maybe he should just throw them away. He'd never really liked that daisy pattern, anyway. He'd picked them up cheap at a local thrift store when money had been tight. Now he could afford more masculine dishes. Maybe something with trucks on it.

While he pondered if he should buy glasses to match, the doorbell rang.

"It's open," he called out, lifting his head and opening his eyes, but not bothering to get up. No reason to aggravate his toe any more than necessary. Maybe it was Kimberly, returning to tell him it was all a big joke.

But he didn't laugh when a sultry brunette strode into his dining room. She wore a stylish turquoise dress that outlined a luscious hourglass figure. The kind of body a man could sink his hands into. With a conscious effort, he lifted his gaze from her dress to look at her face. He noticed her big brown eyes first, fringed with thick, dark lashes, then her pert nose and full pink lips.

This woman was no nun.

So, who was she? And what was she doing in his ranch house? He swallowed hard as a curious mixture of apprehension and desire rose inside of him. But before he could ask her anything, she placed both hands on the table and leaned toward him, unwittingly displaying her generous cleavage. Then she spoke.

"You're just the man I've been looking for."

2

Chloe silently counted to ten while Cade Holden stared at her. Cursed with genes that made all the Galetti women well-endowed, she was used to men paying avid attention to her physical assets and ignoring the fact that she was a savvy, intelligent woman. But this one was different. He obviously appreciated her assets but studied her in a way that seemed to probe into her very soul.

She impatiently cleared her throat to get his attention. It worked. He looked up at her, his eyes slightly glazed. For the first time she noticed their unusual color—a deep, dark blue like polished sapphires. If she put any stock in physical appearance, she'd have to admit this cowboy was good-looking. All right, just plain gorgeous with that square jaw, aquiline nose, and close-cropped dark hair. She couldn't help but notice how well the rest of him looked either, his rock-hard biceps and broad shoulders clearly defined through his black Western shirt.

"You're staring," Cade announced.

"Me?" Chloe swallowed, her throat dry. "You were the one who was staring."

"I always stare at beautiful women. Especially when they suddenly appear out of nowhere." Then his eyes narrowed with suspicion. "Why were you looking for me?"

She motioned toward the empty chair in front of her. "Aren't you going to ask me to sit down?"

"I'd rather you answer my question first. Or maybe I can answer it for you. My grandmother, Hattie Holden, sent you here, didn't she?"

"She gave me your address, but..."

"I knew it," he interjected, shaking his head in disgust. "I knew it was too good to be true."

Chloe pulled out the chair and sat down next to him. "It?"

"I mean you," he muttered, then heaved a long sigh. "Look, we both know why you're here. Let's just skip the preliminaries and get right down to it." He leaned forward, closing the distance between them. "Kiss me."

Her mouth dropped open. She quickly closed it

again before he took it as a sign of encouragement. "Are you crazy?"

"No, just efficient. Once you kiss me, we'll both know if there's any future for our relationship. Although I should warn you that the last woman who kissed me decided to never let another man touch her lips again."

Cade Holden was not only a lunatic, but an incredible egomaniac. She smiled sweetly at him. "Thanks, but I'll pass. I make it a habit not to kiss a man within the first five minutes of meeting him. Just one of my little idiosyncrasies."

"Suit yourself." He leaned back in his chair. "So, tell me, Miss..."

"You can call me Chloe."

"Chloe. Do you make it a habit of going door-to-door looking for romance?"

She blinked. "I think you're confused again, Mr. Holden..."

"Call me Cade." He smiled at her, but there was nothing sweet about it. His expression reminded her of a lion contemplating its next meal. "Maybe I am confused. In fact, you're probably just a delightful figment of my imagination. The pain medication is making me a little woozy."

"Pain medication?" she asked, wondering why she

was surprised. There had to be some logical explanation for his odd behavior.

He winced as he lifted his bare foot up in the air. That's when she noticed he'd had it propped up on a padded chair on the opposite side of the table. His big toe was swathed in white gauze so thick it looked like a lightbulb. Before she could stop herself, she emitted a snort of laughter.

His jaw tightened. "Is something funny?"

"I'm sorry," she said, dissolving into uncontrollable, not to mention undignified, giggles. She took a deep breath and struggled to contain her amusement. "Did you hurt yourself?"

He drew himself up in his chair, obviously offended by her reaction. "My toe was almost amputated by a power saw today. The injury required several stitches."

Chloe stared at his foot in disbelief. "You mean that was the horrendous accident Gino was so upset about? You cut your toe?"

He narrowed his eyes. "You know Gino?"

She didn't like his tone. "Better than anyone. He happens to be my little brother."

Cade closed his eyes. "That explains it."

"Explains what?"

"You're a Galetti. That explains why I've felt uneasy ever since you walked through my front door.

I've heard that wherever Galettis go, disaster soon follows."

She rolled her eyes. "Don't you think that's a bit of an exaggeration? Not all Galettis are troublemakers." Most of them, she admitted to herself, but not all.

"Tell that to my toe."

"Let me see it," she said, standing up and walking over to the chair that held his injured foot. She reached out one hand to unwrap the gauze.

"Don't touch it!"

"I just want to take a look," she replied, ignoring his protest. "Don't be so sensitive. I won't hurt you; I promise."

He gently grabbed her wrist. "Are you a doctor?"

"No, I'm an interior designer. And in my professional opinion, white gauze doesn't go at all with the color of this seat cushion. Didn't the pharmacy have anything in lavender?"

"Very funny," he growled.

"They say laughter is the best medicine."

"I prefer Percocet. Unfortunately, it's wearing off, so I'm not the best company right now. Maybe you could come back tomorrow, Ms. Galetti. Or even better, next year."

Some men just couldn't take a joke. "What I have

to say can't wait until next year. It's about Gino. He's very upset."

"He's upset? I'm the one who's been mutilated."

"Oh, come on. It can't be that bad." She gazed down at his foot. "I'll bet if you took off all that gauze, it would hardly even be noticeable."

A muscle ticked in his jaw. "Fine. Take it off and see for yourself."

Surprised by his acquiescence, she leaned over the chair and began carefully unwinding the gauze. All three yards of it. While she worked, she couldn't help but study Cade's foot. There was something almost intimate about seeing the bare foot of a total stranger up close. His was long and lean, with a high arch. The nails were clean and cut short straight across. There were a couple of faded bruises on the top of his foot, possibly from the saw, but more likely from the hazards of working on a ranch.

"Well, what do you think?"

Chloe thought she was much too interested in this man's foot. She forced her gaze to the big toe in question. A neat row of five tiny black stitches arched across the very tip. "I think you'll make a full recovery. Of course, that's just a layperson's opinion." She bit back a smile. "Have you thought about consulting a specialist?"

Cade carefully set his bare foot on the floor, his

handsome face set in a scowl. "Actually, I'm thinking about calling my attorney. Assault with a deadly weapon happens to be a felony."

She straightened, her amusement fading. "You can't be serious."

"Obviously, you're the one who can't be serious, since you consider this all a big joke."

"It's no joke," she agreed. "In fact, I don't find it the least bit funny that you fired Gino over something this"—she pointed to his toe— "inconsequential."

"I happen to like my big toe," he said through clenched teeth. "And I'd like to keep it. Which means Gino had to go."

Chloe swallowed hard and willed the infamous Galetti temper to stay under control. The last thing she wanted was for Cade to kick her out of his ranch house. Not until she got what she came for. "Just give him one more chance."

"Why should I?"

Because she was terrified her brother would do something crazy if he lost this opportunity. He'd been despondent ever since his fiancée broke up with him —frustrated with his lack of job skills and life in general. Gino wanted a challenge. Excitement. Riches. Lately, he'd even talked about following in their father's footsteps. Gino might be a mediocre carpenter's apprentice, but she knew for certain he'd make one hell of a lousy jewel thief. Which meant if she didn't do something fast, another Galetti would end up behind bars.

"Well?" Cade asked, breaking into her reverie. "Why should I give your brother a second chance to dismember me?"

As she stared into his deep blue eyes, her stomach suddenly went all queasy on her. This cowboy was too self-absorbed, too stubborn, and much too sure of himself to understand how much this job meant to someone as sensitive and insecure as her brother. And she'd be damned if she was going to beg.

"Why?" She tipped up her chin. "Because I can make it worth your while."

He settled back in his chair and gave her a slow, insolent once-over. "What exactly are you offering, Ms. Galetti?"

"Myself."

Cade tipped so far back in his chair, he almost toppled over. He grabbed the edge of the dining room table and pulled himself to an upright position. This couldn't be happening. One moment Kimberly announces she's joining a convent, and the next moment a sexy woman sails into his home and offers herself to him.

He must be dreaming. Or hallucinating. Perhaps the trauma of his accident was finally getting to him. Although, if a minor injury induced this kind of fantasy, he was almost willing to give Gino free access to all his power tools just to see what else might develop.

Almost.

Of course, this was no dream. Chloe Galetti was standing right in front of him. In the delectable flesh. His common sense told him he could never consent to such an agreement. He'd sworn off letting his impulses make bad decisions for him. Decisions that could hurt him—he let his gaze rove over her once again—or someone else.

Cade cleared his throat. "That's an intriguing proposition."

She sat down in the empty chair. "I call it good business. Tit for tat."

He closed his eyes, wishing she hadn't used that particular phrase. When he opened them again, she was still there, sitting with one long, slender leg crossed over the other, her dress barely reaching mid-thigh. He'd never seen legs like hers before. They were true works of art. And he was a devoted connoisseur. He tore his gaze from her legs. "Are you sure you're an interior designer?"

"Positive. And a darn good one, too. That's the reason Cowboy Confidential hired me to decorate that café you're renovating." She hesitated, then one corner of her mouth tipped up in a slow smile. "Or at least, one of the reasons."

"So, I was right!" he exclaimed, confirming his worst fear. "My grandmother did send you here." He'd been after Grandma Hattie for weeks to hire an interior designer for the café. Only she'd chosen a beautiful woman to work with him. And even worse, a Galetti.

The fact that she was a Galetti did give him pause. Surely, even Grandma Hattie wouldn't want him marrying into that crime family and undoing a lot of the progress he'd made since his wild youth. Maybe she'd given up trying to play matchmaker for him. Or more likely, she was getting desperate.

Chloe nodded and opened that sensual mouth, but he interrupted her before she had a chance to elaborate.

"Wait a minute," he said, as the rest of her words finally sank in. "What do you mean, one of the reasons?"

She arched one delicate brow. "You don't know?"

Chloe leaned toward him, her pink tongue darting out to moisten her lips. "No idea at all?"

He shook his head, his throat dry. If he didn't know better, he'd think she was purposely tormenting him. But Chloe could have no idea of the effect she was having on him. Cade had learned to keep his strong emotions to himself. Perhaps Kimberly had resigned herself to life in a convent because he'd become too good at hiding his feelings.

"Interesting." She settled back in her chair. "Because the rumor is that Hattie Holden is quite the matchmaker." Her brown eyes flicked over him. "For some inexplicable reason, she thinks we'd be a perfect couple."

He stared at her. "She actually said that?"

Chloe nodded, then tucked an errant tawny curl behind her ear. "She didn't want to tell me at first, because apparently she believes romance should take its natural course. But then..." Her voice trailed off.

He looked at her. "But then... what?"

"But then she saw how upset I was when I learned you'd fired Gino. I believe I might have even called you a few unsavory names in the heat of the moment."

"Such as?"

She blinked innocently at him. "I'm sure I don't remember."

He was sure she did, but he let her continue the story.

"I was going to quit on the spot, but Hattie convinced me to give you another chance." Chloe smiled. "She's a very determined woman."

Determined was an understatement. She might not literally be able to move mountains, but his grandmother had definitely caused a few avalanches in her time. If she was set on bringing Cade and this Galetti woman together...

He suppressed a shiver, although he knew that same wily determination had saved his butt more than a few times. And one time in particular. If it hadn't been for Grandma Hattie, Cade might not even be sitting here right now, ready to turn down Chloe's incredibly tempting offer.

She seemed nice enough, for a Galetti. And at one point in his life, he would have fit right in with her outlaw kin. But he didn't dare risk such an incendiary connection now—no matter how much he was tempted.

Besides, it was appallingly obvious that she was completely wrong for him. He frowned up at her, mentally listing all her flaws. A sassy mouth. A killer body. A classically beautiful face. A quick temper too, judging by the sparks he'd seen in her big brown eyes. And worst of all, a brother named Gino.

He sat back in his chair with a sigh. No, Chloe didn't fulfill any of the requirements on his list for the perfect wife. But despite her obvious flaws, he found it more difficult to turn her down than he'd expected. "I'm flattered, Ms. Galetti."

"Call me Chloe," she reminded him.

"Chloe," he echoed. "I'm flattered by your very generous offer. I admire your loyalty to your brother and the lengths you're willing to go to help him. But I'm afraid I can't..."

"I'd do anything for Gino," she said, interrupting him once again. "Family loyalty is very important to me."

"Me, too," he muttered. Family loyalty rated very high on Cade's list of wifely requirements. But one positive didn't make up for all the glaring negatives that still tipped the scales against her.

"How important?"

He blinked. "What?"

"Exactly how important is your family to you?"

"What does that have to do with your offer to sleep with me?"

She stared at him. Then the corners of her mouth quivered until she couldn't contain herself any longer and burst out laughing. "Sleep with you?"

He scowled, wondering what was so darn funny. "Yes. In exchange for me hiring back your brother."

"This is too much," she said, her laughter abruptly subsiding. She took a deep breath to compose herself. "Just what kind of woman do you think I am?"

"I... I..."

"And what kind of man," she continued, anger flashing in her eyes, "would even consider using a woman that way?"

This had gone far enough. "I think you misunderstood me. I had no intention..."

"You know," she interjected, "I've met some thickheaded cowboys in my time, but I didn't realize men like you still existed."

"If you would just allow me to get a word in edgewise," he said between clenched teeth, "you'd find out I had absolutely no intention of taking you up on your offer."

But instead of mollifying her, his words seemed to offend her. Sparks lit her eyes. "So not only did you believe I was willing to offer my body to you, but you also have the nerve to sit there and tell me you're not the least bit interested."

"I never said that," Cade growled. "I'm very interested. I'm so interested I can barely sit up straight. In fact, if you'd like me to prove it to you, I'll be more than happy to oblige."

"That won't be necessary," she said primly. "Because I'm definitely *not* interested. Not now, not ever. So can we please return to the subject at hand?"

He was both disappointed and confused. "What subject?"

She settled back in her chair, still bristling, and scowled at him.

As much as he hated to admit it, she was just as appealing to him in the heat of anger. Maybe even more so. A rosy blush stained her creamy cheeks. Her brown eyes sparkled. His own blood raced in anticipation of what she might say or do next.

"Family loyalty," she said at last. "Gino is the only reason I showed up here tonight."

He rubbed one hand over his face. *Gino.* Why did she have to remind him? Although perhaps it was a good thing she had, considering the directions his thoughts had taken just a scant moment ago. She was a Galetti. Which meant she was off-limits.

She tilted her head to one side as she studied him. "The way I see it, we need each other—professionally speaking. Pine City has a shortage of good interior designers and I'm trying to build my resumé. So, are you interested in my proposition?"

"Maybe you'd better explain exactly what you mean by proposition."

"Fine. I'll talk slowly this time, so you understand." She leaned forward. "If you will hire my brother back, I'll offer Cowboy Confidential my interior designer services for free on a future project."

"Be still my heart," he said dryly. "Thanks, but no thanks."

She arched a brow. "I thought you said family loyalty is important to you. Are you really willing to disappoint your grandmother? She was very worried I was going to quit when she heard my tirade against you."

"Tirade? I thought you just called me a couple of names."

"Among other things." She cleared her throat. "The point is, she has her heart set on the two of us working together. Are you willing to break it?"

Chloe couldn't have hit her mark better if she'd drawn a bull's-eye on his chest. The last thing Cade wanted to do was disappoint Grandma Hattie. He owed her. Big-time. Still, he'd sworn to himself not to get matched up with a woman through Cowboy Confidential. And until Chloe walked through his front door, he'd thought he'd succeeded.

"I don't know," he said slowly, studying her face. "Are you sure you're not in this to find a fella?"

"Of course not." She suppressed a shiver. "And your grandmother will eventually realize that we're completely wrong for each other."

"You can say that again."

"We're completely wrong for each other."

He frowned at her. "That was just a figure of speech."

"I know. I just wanted to repeat it in case you once again fall under the delusion that I have any interest in sleeping with you."

Her words pricked him more than he wanted to admit. He'd never had two women so thoroughly reject him in one night before. "Not a problem."

"So do we have a deal?"

His common sense told him to turn her down and turn her out of his ranch house. But his love for his grandmother overrode his better judgment. "Deal."

"Good," she said with a sigh of satisfaction. "I'll tell Gino that he can show up for work first thing in the morning." She rose to her feet and held out her hand. "Shall we shake on it?"

Cade complied, enveloping her smaller, softer hand in his large grasp. The warmth of her skin sent an odd shiver through him, and he was surprised by the strength of her grip. "Give me a chance to call my insurance agent first. I want to increase my acci-dental death-and-dismemberment policy to the max."

"Very funny," she mused, turning toward the front door.

Cade stood up to follow her, momentarily forgetting about his sore toe. "Wait a minute. How exactly will this work?"

She turned around. "What do you mean?"

"How will we convince Grandma Hattie that we're not meant for each other?"

"I think that will soon become obvious to everyone." Then she nibbled her lower lip. "Although, we'll have to pretend to get along at the very least, or your grandmother might replace me. And I have some great design ideas for the café, so I'd rather stay on the job."

"Okay then, we'll need to compare notes. The sooner we get this place ready to go, the sooner we can part ways."

"Perfect. Are you free tomorrow night?" Chloe asked him. "I've got everything set up in my office and I'd rather not haul my designs down to the café while there's still sawdust in the air."

Cade hesitated, not wanting to misunderstand this invitation too. "You're inviting me to your office on a Friday night?"

"Yes, say around eight? I can show you a few of the design plans I've drawn up. And you can bring some takeout for us. We'll go over your blueprints during dinner and brainstorm some ideas."

"Okay, sure." He limped toward her. "No problem."

She smiled up at him. "See, we're working well together already." Pulling a business card out of her purse, Chloe handed it to him. "Here's my home address and cell phone number."

"Home address?" he echoed, taking the card from her. "I thought we were meeting at your office."

"I'm temporarily working out of my house," she clarified. "Setting up a new business takes time and money, so I haven't had a chance to rent office space yet."

He nodded, a feeling of uneasiness stirring deep inside him. She was inviting him to her home. On a Friday night. And asking him to bring dinner. "Okay, got it. What kind of takeout would you like?"

"How about Thai?"

"I don't like Thai food."

She shrugged. "Okay, how about Indian. I love a good curry."

He winced. "Sorry, I'm not a big fan."

"All right," she said with a slight shake of her head. "What would you like to eat?"

"I know a great barbecue place. How do smoked ribs with cornbread and coleslaw sound?"

She smiled. "My favorite combination."

"Mine, too. Seems we have something in common, after all."

"Scary, isn't it?" she quipped, then sailed out the front door.

Cade leaned against the open doorframe and watched her walk toward her car, a sporty red two-door coupe that looked out of place next to his mud-splattered pickup truck. The night air was crisp and cool, making her quicken her steps as she crossed the yard. The way her dress molded to her swaying hips made his mouth go dry. Then realization sank in. He'd be spending every day of the next two to three weeks working with her.

Scary was certainly the word for it.

By Friday, Cade was more than scared; he was downright suspicious. The night before he'd tossed and turned in his bed, unable to sleep, and replayed Chloe's unexpected visit in his mind. The more he thought about it, the more he was convinced she had orchestrated every aspect of their encounter—right down to the alluring shade of lipstick she wore. How else could he explain the fact that he'd agreed to work with Chloe Galetti after vowing to his grandmother that he'd never fall into one of her matchmaking traps?

Then another thought hit him, chilling him to the

very marrow. Maybe Grandma Hattie had planned it this way all along. Asking him to hire Gino, the power-saw incident, Chloe's visit to his ranch and their unusual deal.

"Don't you think you're just a little paranoid?" Jack Holden asked, after Cade had explained his suspicions to his brother. They stood in the large rustic dressing room of Happy Trails Formal Wear.

Cade buttoned his sage-green vest. "You tell me. I'm trying on tuxedos with my recently engaged brother who is getting married next month. And you met your gal through Cowboy Confidential, just like Nick, Hank, and Sam—all thanks to Grandma Hattie."

"I've thanked her more than once." Jack smiled as he knotted his tie. "Carly is the best thing that ever happened to me. You and Trace just need to accept the inevitable."

Cade shrugged into a black tuxedo jacket. "And follow the rest of you into matrimony like lambs to the slaughter?" He shook his head. "Nah, we're not that dumb."

Jack laughed as he slapped his younger brother on the shoulder. "You boys act more like stubborn mules than lambs. You can kick up a fuss all you want, Cade, but you're the one who agreed to work with this Galetti woman and her goofy brother."

"Consider it my wedding gift to you and Carly."

Cade flexed his shoulders, the jacket pulling tightly across his back. He pulled it off and then reached for a larger size from the rack. "Interior designers are hard to come by in Pine City and I'm determined to have the café ready for business by the time you two return from your honeymoon."

"Then why do you look so worried? Apparently, this Chloe is all wrong for you, which is hardly surprising if she's anything at all like her brother."

"She's nothing like Gino." Cade buttoned the jacket, finding the fit just right. "But she's still dangerous. You should see her, Jack. Or maybe not." He grinned. "If you saw Chloe Galetti, you might just decide to remain a bachelor."

The dressing room curtain was suddenly swept open. Carly Weiss, Jack's fiancée, stood on the other side. "Hey, Cade, quit trying to sabotage this wedding." Her voice sounded stern, but her blue eyes sparkled with amusement. "Or I may just have to kill you."

"Carly," Jack whispered, "you're not supposed to be in here. This is the men's dressing room."

She laughed. "Sounds like the perfect place to be to me. Unfortunately, you're both decent." She turned to Cade. "So, who's Chloe?"

"No one for you to worry about," Cade replied, looking fondly at his future sister-in-law. Carly didn't have any competition for his brother's affections. He'd never seen Jack so besotted with a woman.

She smiled up at Cade. "So, I can let you live?"

"You'd better, since I'm the best man. Somebody has to catch Jack when he passes out from a panic attack during the wedding ceremony."

"Ignore him," Jack said, drawing Carly into his arms and giving her a tender kiss on the lips. "If I start to panic, it will only be because it's taking so darn long to make you my wife. It seems like I've been waiting forever."

Carly moved closer to him. "I agree. So why is everyone else calling it a whirlwind romance?" She wrapped her arms around Jack's neck. "I'm ready to start the honeymoon."

Jack responded with another kiss, this one longer than the last. Cade folded his arms across his chest, waiting for them to come up for air. They'd been like this ever since they'd announced their engagement.

As much as Cade hated to admit it, he envied his older brothers. Soon Jack would have exactly what Cade wanted—an adoring woman as his wife. A family of his very own.

He tugged at his silk tie. Not only had the Kimberly fiasco set him back, but now this situation with Chloe would cause an even longer delay. He just wanted a woman who fit all his requirements, who shared all his likes and dislikes, who didn't make him completely crazy.

Was that so much to ask?

He glanced at his watch, then impatiently cleared his throat. "Sorry to interrupt, but you two aren't on your honeymoon yet."

Carly turned to him, her cheeks flushed a becoming pink. "I'm still waiting for you to tell me about Chloe."

"Do you remember me telling you about Gino?" Jack asked her. "He's the guy who almost amputated Cade's toe. Well, she happens to be his sister and is also your café's new interior designer."

Carly clapped her hands with delight as she whirled around to face Cade. "Grandma Hattie finally found someone?"

"She sure did," Cade admitted, "so I guess we're stuck with her."

Carly's brow furrowed. "Stuck with her? Does that mean you think she won't do a good job?"

"It's not that." Cade cleared his throat. "She invited me over to her house tonight and asked that I bring dinner for us. We're supposed to look at her design plans, but..."

"But?" Carly prodded.

"Could this be a date?" Cade blurted out. "I mean, it's dinner at her house on a Friday night. I don't think it's a date, but sometimes I miss a woman's signals."

"Whoa." Carly held up one hand. "A date? What about Kimberly?"

"Kimberly is out of the picture," Jack said, sparing the details. "Chloe is in. Grandma Hattie is playing matchmaker again."

Carly's eyes widened. "Oh, Cade. How wonderful! You've finally met your match."

"You can say that again," Jack said with a chuckle.

"Chloe Galetti is not my perfect match," Cade said firmly. "I'm only doing this for Grandma Hattie. Once she sees how wrong we are for each other, maybe she'll stop trying to interfere in my love life."

Carly looked thoughtful. "You know, it is possible Hattie made a mistake."

"Hey," Jack interjected as he wrapped his arm around her waist. "I thought you were a believer."

"I am," Carly insisted. "But if Cade is afraid to work with Chloe, I'm willing to wait for another interior designer to come along."

"Or he could follow Trace's lead and just skip town." Jack turned to Cade. "Trace got fitted for his tux yesterday and is already on his way to Denver."

"Hey, I'm not going anywhere." Cade's tone was more strident than he intended. Clearing his throat, he spoke more calmly. "Chloe and I made a deal to work together, and I'm a man of my word."

"All right," Carly said with a nod. "I'm glad you're staying put, Cade. But I can see why your little brother isn't sticking around. I was here with Trace when he tried on his tux." She pulled open the dressing room curtain and pointed to the front room. "He looked so handsome that three women came in off the street when they saw him through the window."

"Speaking of handsome," Jack said, holding out his arms and executing a slow turn in his tuxedo. "What do you think?"

She tapped one finger on her chin as she took her time studying her fiancé. Then she turned her analytical eye to Cade. "Well, if you want to know the truth..."

"We can take it," Cade said.

Carly's mouth curved into a sly smile. "Then I'd say Chloe Galetti and I are the two luckiest women in Texas."

3

On Friday evening, Chloe silently fumed as she dressed for her meeting with Cade. She wanted to hit something. Or more specifically, someone. And that someone was her second cousin, Antoinette Galetti, who was the reason Chloe had just lost a job contract with Pine City's largest clothing boutique.

The boutique's owner, a sweet grandmother with a flair for fashion, had been excited to sign Chloe's contract until Antoinette had walked past them in the boutique, escorted by a security officer and wearing a pair of handcuffs. Not only had Antoinette been arrested for shoplifting, but she'd called out to Chloe, asking her 'favorite cousin' for bail money.

The owner had then politely declined Chloe's interior design services. Once again, her family's unsavory reputation had turned off a potential client. Which made tonight's meeting with Cade even more critical. He could still back out of their deal, especially since he seemed so skittish about working with her.

That's why she wanted everything to be perfect. Three months ago, she'd converted the attic into her third-floor office space. She loved the dormer ceiling and sash windows that gave the room a distinctive charm. After cleaning her office from top to bottom, Chloe had set up a small round table with two chairs where they could eat their take-out dinner while discussing their plans for the café. She'd place standing easels near the table to display her design plans and couldn't wait to pore over Cade's blueprints.

A thrill of excitement shot through her. If this café job was a success, maybe her talents as an interior designer would assuage any concerns future clients might have about her felonious family members.

Taking a deep, calming breath, Chloe turned to the full-length mirror in her bedroom. She'd chosen to wear a black jersey dress with matching knee-high boots and delicate silver bangle bracelets for this meeting. The style was classic and professional, and best of all, comfortable. She opened her makeup bag and began searching for her mascara when there was a familiar knock on her bedroom door.

"It's open, Gino. Come on in."

The door opened and she turned to see her brother in the doorway, his face set in a frown. "Chloe, I have something to say to you," Gino began.

"Okay, but can you make it quick?" She dumped the contents of the makeup bag onto her dresser. "Cade is due to arrive any minute."

"That's what I want to talk to you about. With Dad gone, I'm the head of this family now, and I don't like the idea of you dating Cade Holden. I think you should call it off."

"This isn't a date; it's a business meeting." Chloe leaned close to the mirror and carefully applied a touch of mascara to her long dark lashes. "I made you a pot roast with carrots, potatoes, and onions for supper. If you eat all your vegetables, you can have some cookie dough ice cream for dessert."

Gino wrinkled his nose. "You know I don't like your pot roast. Besides, I have plans tonight."

Chloe studied her brother. His shoulder-length brown hair was slicked back into a neat ponytail. He wore a blue pinstripe shirt and crisply pressed denim blue jeans. He'd shaved recently too, judging by the small tuft of toilet paper stuck to his chin. "What kind of plans?"

He shrugged. "I'd rather not say." Then his brown eyes widened in dismay. "And you changed the subject. We were talking about Holden."

She turned back to the mirror, able to see his reflection in the glass. "What about him?"

"He's not your type, Chloe. Believe me, I know. I've heard he even has a list of requirements for the perfect wife."

"Don't worry, Gino," she said with a laugh. "I have no interest in that job."

"Well, I still forbid you to have dinner with him. I don't trust the man, and I certainly don't like him. He wouldn't let me handle any of his precious tools at work today." His mouth drew down in a pout. "Nothing except the broom."

Chloe feared her brother was following his usual pattern of taking a new job and then quitting when things didn't go the way he wanted. She was still amazed he'd lasted as a barista for six whole months. But this job with Cade had real potential and didn't require a college degree. He just needed to give it a chance.

"You're a carpenter's apprentice," Chloe reminded him. "You've got to start somewhere. I'm sure Cade will give you access to more tools as you gain some experience."

"I don't have that much time," Gino said, shaking

his head. "I'm already twenty-two years old."

"You're still a spring chicken, as Dad used to say." She smiled at the memory. "Don't worry, Gino, you have a few good years left."

"I'm serious, Chloe. Life is passing me by. And what do I have to show for it? Nothing. Zilch. Nada." He took a deep breath. "It's time for me to make some big changes."

The hairs prickled on the back of her neck. "What kind of big changes?"

"Hey, you changed the subject again. We were talking about you and Cade."

She turned to face him, a tube of raspberry-red lipstick in her hand. "Right now, we're talking about you. I want to know exactly what kind of changes you're planning to make."

"It's a secret."

She took a step toward him. "Gino, please don't do anything foolish."

"What's that supposed to mean?"

"We both know what it means. I realize the past few years have been rough on you. Especially after Dad died." She didn't want to admit they'd been rough on her too. The sudden death of Lorenzo Galetti eight years ago had left Chloe, a naive nineteen-year-old, in sole charge of her emotional fourteen-year-old brother. She'd tried her best to raise him right, with plenty of unsolicited advice from her incarcerated mother and assorted Galettis.

"I really miss him," Gino admitted. "He was my hero."

Just the words she didn't want to hear. "I loved Dad, too. But he had his faults. He was too smart to waste his life cracking safes. He could have done so much more."

Gino's eyes sparked with anger. "Lorenzo Galetti was the best jewel thief in the country. That's how he supported our family and bought this house. The cops never even came close to touching him."

"Yes, I know," she said softly. "But the stress of evading the authorities all those years took its toll. He was only forty-seven when his heart gave out."

Gino's shoulders drooped. "The same thing could have happened if he'd been a plumber or a banker. Besides, he loved his work."

Sometimes Chloe wondered if her father had loved his work more than he'd loved his family. Growing up, they'd never been able to stay in one place long—making it necessary for Chloe and Gino to change schools often. They'd had to lie, too, whenever anyone asked them about what Lorenzo did for a living. Their parents had told them the secret to a good lie was mixing a little truth in with the fiction you were trying to sell.

He's in the security business had been Chloe's standard reply when anyone asked her about her father. Only she'd refrained from mentioning that his specialty was finding ways to break into sophisticated security systems and steal the goods.

Chloe had hated lying to friends and neighbors, often living life in the shadows. That's why she'd vowed to never follow in her family's criminal footsteps.

Still, it hadn't been a bad childhood. The Galettis were a close-knit family, and they'd always been able to depend on each other. Which was the reason Chloe was not going to let her brother down, whether he wanted her help or not.

"Times are different now," she said briskly, turning back to the mirror. "The police have all kinds of high-tech equipment to track stolen merchandise. So, if you're thinking of taking up where Dad left off, think again."

The doorbell rang, forestalling Gino's reply. But she could see by the mottled flush on his cheeks that she'd hit a nerve. "That must be Cade."

"I'll get it," Gino said, moving toward the doorway.

Chloe picked up a pair of silver hoop earrings off the top of her dresser and hooked one through her ear. "Tell him I'll be down in a minute."

"I will," Gino called over his shoulder. "And I'll tell him a few other things, too."

She rolled her eyes at his retreating back, then put on the other earring. Taking one last look in the mirror, Chloe ran her fingers lightly through her hair, surprised by the fluttery sensation in the pit of her stomach. Despite their rocky start, she wanted to make a good impression on Cade. If she was successful, his work as a contractor would make him a great reference for future design jobs. The tricky part was maintaining a professional relationship with the man while his grandmother was pushing for a romantic one.

Fortunately, Cade had made it clear that he wasn't interested in a romance with her. It was a good thing, too. Because despite her skepticism about Hattie Holden's matchmaking abilities, she couldn't deny a strange pull between them. There was something about that cowboy that unsettled her. Something that almost made her forget she didn't even like the man.

Cade broke out in a cold sweat as he stood waiting on the wraparound porch of the rambling Victorian house. He held a big bag of smoked ribs in one hand and blueprints for the café in the other. He'd been restless all day, wavering between apprehension and anticipation. The prospect of this business meeting with Chloe Galetti intrigued him and unnerved him at the same time. Now that the moment had finally arrived, he didn't know whether he should ring the doorbell again or take off running in the opposite direction.

Trace's warning echoed in his mind. *Be afraid, Cade. Be very afraid.* Then he shook off the words as well as his sense of foreboding. Cade Holden had never let fear dictate to him before, and he wasn't about to start now.

Besides, it was a simple business meeting. How bad could it be?

The front door swung open. Gino stood on the other side, a scowl on his face and a six-inch carving knife in his left hand. "Oh, it's you."

"Put the knife down, Gino."

Gino held the knife up in the air, the silver blade glinting in the glow of the porch light. "This little thing? I was just using it to slice up a roast."

"Put it down, Gino," Cade repeated, more sternly this time. After almost losing his big toe, he wasn't about to take any chances.

Gino's eyes flashed with anger, but he took a step back. "And what if I don't?"

Cade moved a step closer to the threshold. "Then

I'll have to take it away from you, and you won't like the way I do it."

Gino hesitated a moment, then dropped the knife into the potted plant just inside the front door. The hilt quivered slightly as the blade neatly pierced the soil. "All right, have it your way."

"Thank you." Cade waited for him to move away from the open doorway. "May I come in now?"

Gino stood with his hands on his narrow hips, partially blocking his path. "Could I stop you?"

"No," Cade said genially, moving past him as he stepped across the threshold and into the living room. He set down his cowboy hat on a small table near the front door, along with his blueprints and the bag of ribs. Then he looked around the room. "Is Chloe here?"

"I told her to wait upstairs so we could have a little chat." Gino turned to face him. "Exactly what are your intentions toward my sister?"

"I simply intend to share a basket of ribs with her and discuss design plans for the café. This is a business meeting."

Gino rolled his eyes. "Yeah, that's what she keeps saying, too. But I'm not worried about dinner. I want to know what you have in mind for dessert."

"Something sweet and soothing, which pretty much rules out your sister." Then he smiled. "Don't worry about it, Gino. I'm not interested in Chloe that way." Which wasn't exactly true, but he didn't like the way Gino was still eyeing that knife.

"I hope not." Gino moved a step closer to him, the top of his head barely reaching Cade's chin. "Because otherwise you'll have to answer to me."

"Thanks for the warning," Cade said dryly.

"Please remember it," Gino said, attempting a menacing glare. "Oh, and can I have tomorrow off?"

"Nope, you need to be at the café at seven o'clock sharp."

Gino sighed, all his bravado instantly deflating. "Okay, I'll try to make it, but I have to stop for coffee first or I'll be useless to you." Then he turned on his heel and strode out of the living room, his footsteps echoing on the hardwood floor as he disappeared into another part of the house.

Cade watched him leave, grudgingly impressed with Gino's efforts to watch out for his sister. The man might be kind of a nut, but he was a loyal nut.

Left on his own, Cade could finally feast his eyes on the exquisitely crafted and spacious front living room. There were two vintage chandeliers, dripping with sparkling crystals. It also boasted two fireplaces, a high ceiling, and a breathtaking grand staircase. He saw evidence of fine workmanship everywhere he looked. Intricate crown moldings, arched entryways, and original mantels made his heart beat faster.

The largest arched window, reaching from floor-to-ceiling, was a showpiece, accented with rose, amber, and green stained glass. Marble insets flanked the hand-carved windowsill and adorned both fire-places. The vintage sofa and armchairs fit perfectly in the room, sharing the same colors found in the stained glass. He noticed Chloe's purse sitting atop an antique glass door that had been repurposed into a gorgeous coffee table.

Cade stared in wonder around the rest of the unique room, touching each surface with an almost breathless reverence. Chloe obviously wasn't his perfect match, but he was falling hard and fast for her beautiful home.

He had to give her credit, though. She'd decorated it just right. The simple, tasteful furnishings and decor enhanced rather than detracted from the detailed carpentry work and the nineteenth-century grandeur of the setting. Chloe had also used a playful mix of solid and print fabrics to lighten the mood of the room and give it a welcoming air. He just hoped she could do half as well with Carly's new café.

Saving the best for last, Cade moved toward the curved, oak staircase. He'd never seen a staircase like this up close before, although he knew a handful had been built in Pine City in the 1890s. It was much wider and sturdier than any modern-day staircase. Trimmed with raised wood panels, it featured elegant balustrades and elaborately carved newel posts. The staircase was in amazing condition for its age, the solid oak gleaming and polished to a high sheen. Unable to resist, he reached out one hand and ran it down the smooth handrail. He didn't know enough about real estate to guess the value of the old house, but the staircase itself had to be worth a fortune.

He wondered who had built it. One of his hobbies was studying the techniques of local craftsmen from the nineteenth and early twentieth centuries. They had built some of the finest houses in Texas. He bent down to look at the underside of the staircase, hoping to find a date or even hand-carved initials of the person responsible for this masterpiece.

He saw something far different.

"What the hell?" he muttered, angling his head for a better view. Then he heard footsteps behind him. But before he could turn around, something solid and heavy struck his temple. He blinked in surprise as a blinding pain streaked through his head.

Then everything went black.

Chloe finished answering a string of text messages from a potential client before finally leaving her bedroom to meet with Cade. The sound of a loud thud from below made her pause at the top of the staircase. "Gino?"

No answer. It was quiet down there. Too quiet. She hoped Gino hadn't refused to let Cade inside the house. Or maybe the man hadn't shown up at all. In the past twenty-four hours, she'd wondered more than once if Cade would want to back out of their deal.

Her doubts turned to uneasiness when she reached the first-floor landing. The living room was empty, but the front door stood wide open. She walked toward it and looked outside. The covered front porch stood empty too, although Cade's freshly washed pickup truck was parked on the street out front.

Chloe closed the door and turned back into the living room. That's when she saw the hilt of a large knife sticking out of the potted plant. It looked as if someone had tried to murder her bamboo palm.

"Gino?" she called out again, carefully pulling the knife out of the yellow ceramic pot, her gaze scanning the empty living room. "Where are you?"

Then the mouthwatering aroma of barbecue hit her, and she saw a large sack emblazoned with the words Ray's Rib Joint sitting atop the marble accent table. That, along with his pickup truck, meant Cade had to be here somewhere.

She carefully set the knife down and then moved to a side window, where she saw her brother's beat-up '07 hatchback sitting in the narrow driveway.

"Gino?" she called out again, much louder this time as she walked quickly down the long hallway, checking all the other rooms on the main floor. Could Cade possibly have gone upstairs without her seeing him? It seemed unlikely since he wouldn't know the way to her office, but where else could he be?

Chloe moved back into the living room and headed toward the grand staircase, a vague uneasiness settling over her. She'd only climbed a few steps when she looked down and saw the cowboy boots. She blinked in surprise, then leaned over the right side of the banister. Sticking out from under the staircase were a pair of black cowboy boots, the toes pointing up toward the ceiling. She leaned farther and saw that the boots were connected to a pair of long legs clad in blue jeans.

"Cade?" She bounded down the stairs and rounded the newel post, her knees hitting the hard-wood floor right next to the boots. Bending down far enough to peer underneath the staircase, she saw

Cade Holden, unconscious and crammed in the narrow space between the floor and the bottom of the staircase.

His face looked ghostly white in the shadows.

She grabbed one of his legs and shook it. "Cade, are you all right?"

He didn't react to either her voice or her jostling. He just lay there deathly still. Her heart pounded in her chest as panic consumed her. She stood, grabbing both legs this time, and pulled with all her might. His large body moved only a few inches. She tugged on him again, grunting aloud with her effort. He was so impossibly heavy. She'd never moved over two hundred pounds of dead weight before. Dead. The awful word reverberated in her head.

He couldn't be dead. Could he?

At last, she'd pulled his body clear of the staircase. She dived to her knees again and clasped him by the shoulders. "Cade, please wake up. Please!"

The skin at his temple was mottled a dusky blue, and a thin red streak of blood ran down his cheek. His face was still pale, his lips almost bloodless. She wasn't sure he was breathing.

"Cade!" She shouted his name, her throat straining with effort and fear. She called out to him again. Then a third time.

No response.

Frantic now, she cupped one hand under his neck, tilting his chin up. His mouth fell open, revealing a straight line of white teeth. She took a deep breath, then clamped her mouth over his. Exhaling slowly, she tried to fill his lungs with air. But somehow, it wasn't working right.

Then he moved. His lips, anyway, gently molding themselves against her mouth. His tongue darted forward, and her eyes opened wide as it slid sleekly inside.

His eyes were still closed, and she heard a low rumble deep in his throat. Then his hands reached up to cradle her face, holding her gently in place. Pure sensation overcame her shock as his mouth pressed against hers. His fingers trailed down the length of her neck, making her moan softly as his thumbs began stroking her collarbone. Then his hands moved over her shoulders, drawing her even closer to him.

He groaned again. Only this time it sounded more like a groan of pain than pleasure.

Chloe broke the kiss and sat up, watching him grimace as he slowly brought one hand to his temple. She swallowed hard. "You're not dead."

"Obviously." His voice sounded weak and raspy. "What the hell happened?"

"I don't know. I came down here and found you unconscious under the stairs."

His gaze focused on her. "Where exactly is here?"

"My house." She leaned forward, worried he might have a concussion. "I'm Chloe, remember? Chloe Galetti. We have a meeting about the café."

"That's right... Chloe." He closed his eyes. "I dreamed you were kissing me."

It seemed like a dream to her, too. She'd never been kissed like that before. It wasn't just his technique. The man had been barely conscious, after all. It was the unusual spark that had arced between them—connected them.

He opened his eyes. "Or was it all a dream?"

"No. But it wasn't exactly a kiss, either—at least it didn't start out that way." She licked her lips. "That's not important right now. How do you feel?"

"Like someone walloped me with a fence post. What happened?"

"I think you were attacked by a Chihuahua."

He shook his head as if to clear it, then winced. "Am I hearing things? Did you say a Chihuahua?"

She stooped to pick up the small ceramic dog lying upended beneath the stairs. Someone had obviously left it there after hitting Cade in the head with it. One ceramic ear had been chipped off, and the remaining fragment was stained with a small amount of blood. She held it up for him to see. "This used to be Gino's pet, since he's allergic to animal dander. Now we use it for a doorstop."

"It also makes a handy guard dog," he said, gingerly fingering his injury. "I just wish I'd seen it coming."

"What, exactly, were you doing under the staircase?"

"The staircase," he echoed, closing his eyes once more. "Nice. Nice staircase. I wanted to look under it."

She wondered if he was still confused. "Why?"

His brow crinkled as if he was trying to remember the reason. At last, he said, "Names. I was looking for names."

Names? That didn't make any sense. Which shouldn't surprise her since he was suffering from a head injury. "Speaking of names, do you happen to remember yours?"

He opened his eyes and scowled up at her. "Of course."

"Tell me," she said, wanting to be certain.

"Cade Joseph Holden. I'm twenty-nine years old and live on Elk Creek Ranch." He arched a brow, then winced at the slight movement. "Am I right?"

"The name and place are right, but you look older than twenty-nine."

"At the moment, I feel about eighty-nine." He

struggled to sit up, his face blanching at the effort. "Make that ninety-nine."

She clasped his broad shoulder and helped pull him up to a sitting position. He closed his eyes, then slowly dropped his head between his knees.

"Give me a minute," he said. "The room is spinning."

Chloe nibbled her lower lip, wondering if she should call him an ambulance. "Are you sure you're all right? Do you need a doctor?"

After a long moment, he raised head and looked around the room. "I think I'm good. The dizziness has passed."

"I still don't understand what happened."

He glanced over at her. "Isn't it obvious?"

"No, not to me." She stood up and began to pace. "I find you unconscious under the staircase and I can't find my brother anywhere." She paused to look at him, twisting her fingers together. "Do you think Gino is in trouble?"

"Definitely." He gripped the newel post, then rose unsteadily to his feet. "Attempted murder is a serious matter."

Her brow furrowed. "What are you saying?"

"I'm saying that Gino is a danger to himself and others. And I seem to be his number one target." The color was coming back into his face. He looked almost normal but sounded paranoid.

"I think you should sit down again."

"Your brother answered the front door with a carving knife in his hand," he continued, ignoring her advice, "making it perfectly clear that he doesn't want me anywhere near you. Then he attacked me with that Chihuahua." Cade took a couple of wobbly steps in her direction. "And just the other day, he assaulted me with a power saw."

"That was an accident. And this is preposterous. Gino would never... could never... hurt anyone." Her gaze flicked to his foot. "Not on purpose, anyway."

"Chloe, I admire your loyalty, but this is pushing it a bit too far. The man is a menace. He belongs behind bars."

Her blood turned to ice at his words. Gino would never survive in jail. He could barely survive out of jail.

"I know he's your brother," Cade continued, his tone gentler now. "But I have to report him to the police. Otherwise, he's liable to kill someone with these crazy antics. And since I seem to be his favorite target, I'm thinking that someone will be me."

"You don't understand," she breathed. "He's had a tough life. Our family is... different."

A muscle twitched in his jaw. "I do understand—

better than you think. But Gino has to take responsibility for his actions. And a lousy childhood or a lawbreaking family aren't excuses he can hide behind."

His words transformed her fear to anger. "Look, this is ridiculous. I'm telling you that Gino did not knock you out with that Chihuahua. I give you my word."

Cade folded his arms across his chest. "Then who did?"

She shrugged, her mind racing to come up with a plausible suspect. "Well, there's Uncle Vince. Sometimes he drops by unexpectedly. Vince likes to hit first and ask questions later. Then there's Frankie."

"Frankie?"

"My cousin. He works as an enforcer for a loan shark. Sometimes he likes to practice on unsuspecting victims."

"Charming family," he quipped. "Gino is starting to sound better all the time. Any other violent types?"

"Valentina," she replied with a sigh of regret. "Another cousin. She's hated men ever since her high school sweetheart squealed on her to the Feds."

Cade set his jaw. "You really expect me to buy all this?"

"It's the truth." She lifted her chin. "If you don't believe me, call my mother and ask her."

"Maybe I will. Especially if she can talk some sense into you." He pulled his cell phone out of his pocket. "What's her number?"

"One-four-two-three-seven-six."

He arched a disbelieving brow. "That's her telephone number?"

"No, it's her inmate ID number. You'll need it when you call the North Texas Women's Correctional Center."

Cade's eyebrows shot up. "Your mother is...?"

"She's a convicted felon," Chloe said evenly. After her father's death, she'd promised herself not to lie about her family anymore. Honesty kept the shame and embarrassment at bay, but the way Cade was staring at her made her uneasy. "The speed-dial number for the prison is taped on the back of the telephone receiver."

Cade walked over to the vintage telephone stand, where they kept the only landline phone in the house. "You've got three prisons listed here."

"The Galettis get around. And there's a fourth number in the drawer. That one's for the county's juvenile detention center. My uncle Leo's stepson, Benson, recently hot-wired a car on his fifteenth birthday and went joyriding."

Cade kept staring at the speed-dial list. "Your mother is really in prison?"

Chloe heard both surprise and pity in his voice. She didn't care for either. "Yes. But I'm hoping she'll be out on parole in a few weeks."

He turned to her. "Exactly how many Galettis are behind bars?"

Chloe glanced up at the ceiling as she mentally calculated the number. "Currently, there are six, if you count Benson. But he's not technically behind bars. It's more like a very secure rehabilitation facility."

"Six," he echoed.

"So, you see," she said, lifting her chin. "I do have some experience with criminal behavior. Gino just doesn't have it in him, no matter how much he might wish otherwise."

His eyes narrowed. "What does that mean?"

"Nothing," she bit out, wishing she'd bitten her tongue instead. Cade already thought badly enough of her brother without knowing he aspired to become a master jewel thief.

"Tell me."

"It's not important," she insisted, wishing he'd drop it already.

He just stared at her, waiting for her to elaborate.

Was that empathy she saw in his dazed blue eyes? Compassion?

"Fine," she said at last. "On one condition."

"You're hardly in any position to make conditions. You can either tell me right now or I pick up this telephone and call the police."

So much for compassion.

"Go ahead and call them," she bluffed. "I'm not telling you anything."

But instead of reaching for the telephone, Cade walked to the nearest armchair and sat down. He leaned his head back and closed his eyes, his face still unnaturally pale. In that moment, she regretted arguing with him when he had a head injury. She knew in her heart Gino wouldn't purposely hurt anyone, but someone had definitely hurt Cade. And there was a high probability that someone was a Galetti. Pangs of guilt and regret shot through her.

"Can I get you anything?" she asked, her tone softer now. "Some aspirin, or maybe an ice pack for your head?"

"No, thank you," he breathed, his eyes still closed. "I'm just... thinking."

No doubt he was questioning his deal with her, never imagining it would be this dangerous. But she literally couldn't afford for him to back out of it now. Vowing to herself that she would keep him safe,

Chloe grappled for a good reason to make him stay. "How about if I fix you a plate of those ribs?" she offered. "Or I could make you some soup, if that sounds better to you."

He cracked open one eye. "You cook?"

"Since I was twelve." She smiled. "Someone had to take over the meals after Mom went to prison the first time. My father had some antiquated ideas about men staying out of the kitchen, so that left it to me."

"Twelve years old." Cade sighed, both of his eyes open now. "I was five when my parents were killed in a car accident."

"Oh, I'm so sorry," Chloe said, seeing the flash of grief in his eyes.

"Thanks, but my five brothers and I were lucky in a way, I guess." He sat up in the chair. "Grandma Hattie and Grandpa Henry took us in and loved us unconditionally. Even when we messed up." His mouth quirked up in a sheepish smile. "And believe me, I did plenty to make myself unlovable when I was younger."

"Then you understand why I still love my family," she said gently, wondering if Cade would have shared such a vulnerable time in his life if he hadn't been injured. "They're a little on the shady side, but they're all I've got."

"A little?"

"All right," she conceded. "A lot. Except Gino. He's simply not a violent person."

She waited for Cade to contradict her, but he didn't say anything. Maybe she'd convinced him. Maybe he'd already changed his mind about calling the police.

But somebody deserved to pay for attacking Cade. Anger flared inside of her. When she found the Galetti who blindsided him with that Chihuahua, she'd string him, or her, up by their toes. On second thought, she'd do something even worse—she'd make the culprit eat her cooking. Cade had asked her if she could cook, not if she was a good cook. In her case, there was a big difference.

Only she couldn't do anything until she knew what Cade planned to do. Would he press charges against her brother? Or would he finally believe her assertion that Gino was innocent?

"Chloe," he said at last, with the tone of a man who has come to a decision.

"Yes, Cade?" She held her breath, awaiting his verdict.

"There's something else you should know."

4

Cade knew he shouldn't tell Chloe Galetti anything but goodbye. Especially since he'd sincerely underestimated the damage she could do in his life. His pounding head was a powerful reminder of that. He needed to concentrate on his pain, rather than the apprehension he saw in her big brown eyes.

"Something else?" she said, nipping her lower lip between her teeth. "What is it?"

Leave.

The word reverberated in his woozy brain. He could get up right now and leave her behind without a word. This was Galetti family business, after all. No one had asked him to interfere. In fact, he should probably take that blow to the head as a hint to butt out.

So why wasn't he moving?

She walked over to his chair and lightly brushed her fingertips over his forearm. "Tell me, Cade. What else should I know?"

She should know that he never would have agreed to work with her if he hadn't been so desperate to find an interior designer for the café. She should know that he didn't like to interfere in other people's problems. He'd had enough problems in his own past to deal with. She should know that she wasn't responsible for the actions of her brother or her family. That he didn't really blame her for any of this.

She should know... the truth.

"It's about the staircase," he began.

Her brows drew together. "What does the staircase have to do with Gino?"

Instead of replying, he stood up, his knees wobbling and almost giving out. Chloe was immediately standing by his side, lightly supporting him with her body. He closed his eyes for a moment just to enjoy the sensation.

He knew it wouldn't last long.

"Cade, I really think you should lie down. You took a nasty blow, and you're not making a lot of sense right now."

"You'll understand soon enough," he said, feeling stronger now as he walked slowly toward the staircase.

She stayed close beside him, still partially supporting him. "Understand what?"

He could hear the apprehension mingled with impatience in her voice. Hardly surprising. This woman had obviously endured a lifetime of unpleasant revelations—usually about her own family. And he was about to add one more to the list.

"Lie down," he said, when they reached the staircase. He placed one hand on the thick newel post to steady himself.

"What did you say?" She looked at him like he was crazy.

"Lie down on the floor." He reached up to gingerly touch the tender wound on his head. At least it had stopped bleeding.

Worry swam in her brown eyes. "You're not making sense, Cade. I think you're the one who should lie down, but not on the floor." She wrapped one hand around his waist, trying to turn him. "Let's go sit on the nice, cozy sofa."

But he stood his ground. "Just lie down on the floor," he insisted. "Then scoot underneath the staircase and position yourself just as you found me."

With one last look of bewilderment, Chloe acceded to his wishes. She got down on the hardwood floor, then laid on her back and wiggled herself underneath the grand staircase.

Cade waited, his body tensing. He didn't know what he expected to hear. A scream? A curse? A sob? Instead, he heard the one thing he didn't expect—silence. Her reaction, or rather the lack of one, made him wonder if he'd imagined it all in the first place.

"Well?" he asked, bending down slightly, but still unable to read her face in the dim light. "Do you see anything under there?"

Chloe shot out from under the staircase and jumped to her feet. "I certainly do. The dust bunnies have been breeding like rabbits." Then she glanced at her watch. "Okay, should we head upstairs to my office now? I can't wait to see your blueprints."

Her false cheeriness confirmed for Cade that he hadn't imagined it. "It's still there, isn't it?"

Chloe didn't quite meet his gaze. "I didn't see anything out of the ordinary."

With a sigh of resignation, he lumbered down onto the floor himself, ignoring her protests. Then he grabbed the bottom edge of the staircase and slowly pulled himself underneath it. His head throbbed with every movement, but his eyes saw everything clearly. Taped to the underside of the stairwell was a sealed Ziploc gallon bag filled with dozens of sparkling loose diamonds, all shapes and sizes. Even in the shadows underneath the stairs, the jewels winked at him like stars in the sky.

The next moment, Chloe slid in beside him, her back on the floor and her head right next to his. She tilted her gaze toward him. "I can explain."

He couldn't wait to hear it. Would she tell him the truth or make up an elaborate lie? And would he be able to tell the difference? "I'm listening."

She hesitated. "All right, I can't explain. But that doesn't mean there's not a perfectly logical explanation."

"Such as?"

"Such as... these aren't what they look like."

He motioned to the bag above them. "They look like flawless diamonds worth hundreds of thousands of dollars."

"They could just be really good fakes. Sometimes you can hardly tell the difference."

Cade stared at the bag, considering her argument. He supposed they could be fake, but that brought up another question. "If that's true, then why did someone go to all the trouble to hide them?"

"Well... maybe someone is fencing them as the real thing. I admit, they do look authentic."

"I guess there's only one way to find out." As soon as he said the words, he felt her stiffen beside him.

"I don't think that's a good idea."

He turned slightly to get a better view of her face. "You haven't even heard what I have in mind yet."

She frowned. "I can make a wild guess. You want to take them to a jeweler so he can examine them and give us an expert's opinion. Or did you have something else in mind?"

"No, that about sums it up." He rose up onto one elbow. "At least then we'd know what we're dealing with here."

"We?" she echoed, her tone slightly sarcastic. "This isn't your problem, cowboy. This is my house and my staircase."

"And your diamonds?"

When she didn't deny it, the hairs prickled on the back of his neck. Cade hadn't even considered the possibility that Chloe could be involved in something shady. He suddenly wondered why he'd been so blind to that possibility. Was it the way she looked? Talked? Kissed?

But he knew the reason. Grandma Hattie had given Chloe Galetti her unspoken seal of approval when she'd arranged to match Chloe up with Cade. Was it possible his wise grandmother could be so wrong about someone?

He closed his eyes for a moment, not wanting to think about that possibility. Or that strange kiss they'd shared under the stairs. It confused him too much and made perfectly clear issues suddenly seem so cloudy.

The distinctive sound of duct taping ripping made him open his eyes just in time to see Chloe free the bag from the bottom of the staircase.

"They're not my diamonds," she said firmly, holding the bag against her chest. "But this is a Galetti family problem, so you don't need to be involved."

"It's too late. I became involved the moment your brother conked me over the head. And now we know why. He didn't want me to find his stash."

"That's pure speculation," Chloe replied, although she didn't sound convinced. "We don't know who brought these diamonds into the house or how long they've been here. Maybe they've been hidden here for years. I've never had any reason to look under the staircase before."

"Well, somebody knew they were here and this bump on my head is proof of that. It's got to be Gino, since he had the motive, means, and opportunity."

"Gino might have known about the diamonds," Chloe admitted, "but that doesn't mean he's the one who stole them. My father was a master jewel thief. It makes more sense that he hid the diamonds here years ago as some kind of secret insurance policy. A way to make sure his family would be taken care of if anything happened to him."

It was nice fantasy, Cade thought to himself, but

not logical. "I haven't known your brother long, but I can't see him keeping that secret. And how long has your father been gone?"

"Eight years."

He shook his head. "I'm sorry, Chloe, but the simplest explanation is usually the right one."

Chloe set her jaw. "But then why didn't he, or whoever hit you, just take the diamonds and run?"

Cade shrugged. "Maybe Gino heard you coming and panicked. Or maybe he thought he'd killed me and panicked. Criminals aren't always logical. Or smart."

"Believe me, I know." She studied his face for a long moment. "So now what?"

They were lying so close together that he could feel her soft breath on his cheek. "We call the police."

Chloe immediately wiggled out from beneath the staircase. Cade followed her, moving more slowly. She was pacing back and forth in front of the coffee table by the time he got to his feet. He watched her for a moment, then pulled his cell phone out of his pocket.

"Wait," she cried, reaching out to stop him.

He turned to face her. "Chloe, I understand why you're upset. I know you don't want to face the facts about your brother. But shielding Gino won't help. He will just dig himself deeper and deeper into trouble. Believe me, I've been there."

Cade took a step closer to her, his heart softening at the stricken expression on her face. "I'm furious with Gino for knocking me out, but I could handle that with him one-on-one and leave the police out of it."

He steeled himself against the way her brown eyes filled with hope. "However, the diamonds are a different story. We're talking about a serious felony. We don't have any choice but to turn him in to the authorities."

"You're right."

He blinked, surprised at her easy capitulation. Then Chloe moved in quickly and snatched the cell phone out of his hand before he could even react.

"But we don't have to turn him in yet. I still don't believe Gino hit you with the Chihuahua, but..." Her voice trailed off and he saw a spark of anger flash in her eyes.

"You do believe he stole the diamonds?"

"Of course I do," she cried out in anguish. "I'm loyal, not stupid." She cupped her face in her hands, squeezing her eyes shut. "Why couldn't Gino have started small? A gold bracelet here, a semiprecious stone there? Instead, he steals enough diamonds to land him in prison for a lifetime."

"Wait a minute," he interjected, slightly confused.

"Did Gino tell you he planned to become a jewel thief?"

Chloe opened her eyes and looked up at him. "Not in so many words, but I could see the warning signs. Gino worshipped our father and wanted to follow in his footsteps." Her breath caught in her throat. "Why didn't I try harder to stop him?'

"You can't blame yourself." The tears shining in her eyes made him want to reach out and comfort her, but he held himself back.

"But I do blame myself," she told him. "I promised my mother I'd look after Gino the first time she went to prison. And I've tried to keep that promise ever since."

His gut clenched at her words. She'd only been twelve years old when she'd taken on the heavy responsibilities of an adult. "Gino is a man now, not a little boy. You're not responsible for his actions anymore."

"He's still a little boy inside. Sensitive and impulsive." She laid her hand on Cade's chest. "Let me find him. Let me try to convince Gino to turn himself in. Maybe they'll go easier on him then."

Cade shook his head, trying to ignore the way she was touching him. "The police could be on his trail right now. And I'll bet they're definitely on the trail of those diamonds. If they find them here, you could be considered an accomplice."

She squared her shoulders. "I can take care of myself."

Cade knew it wasn't a bluff. She was a strong, independent woman. And he couldn't resist the raw appeal in her unwavering gaze.

"Twenty-four hours," he clipped. "I'll give you twenty-four hours to find your brother. Then we go to the police."

"Thank you!" She threw her arms around his neck, hugging him. "You won't regret it—I promise."

He didn't regret it. Not at this very moment, with Chloe warm and pliant in his arms. He lowered his head and captured her mouth with his, hearing her tiny gasp of surprise. Wrapping his arms around her waist, he pulled her closer, relishing the way her body molded so easily against his own. Seeking an answer to the question that had plagued him ever since she'd tried to give him mouth-to-mouth resuscitation. Now he knew for certain.

It hadn't been a fluke.

The same strange current arced between them—making him feel almost as if their souls were connecting as well as their lips and their bodies. It exhilarated him—and terrified him.

He finally broke the kiss, pressing his cheek

momentarily against her silky hair while he regained control of his equilibrium and his breathing. "I've never attended a business meeting quite like this before."

She laughed, sounding a little breathless herself. Then she stepped out of his arms. "It was short, but memorable."

He frowned. "Does that mean it's over?"

Chloe nodded. "If I only have twenty-four hours to find Gino, I need to begin looking for him right now."

"Do you even know where to start?"

She picked up her purse from the coffee table. "Ducky's Bar on Bale Street. That's one of Gino's favorite hangouts."

"Bale Street?" he echoed in disbelief. "You can't go down to that part of town alone at night. It's bad enough in the daylight."

She slung the purse strap over her shoulder. "I'll be all right. And you should go home and put some ice on your head. I can drop you off if you're not up to driving."

"I'm fine, and I'm going with you." He pulled his pickup truck keys out of his pocket and headed toward the door. "I'll drive."

She hurried to catch up with him. "I really think I should handle this on my own."

He glanced back at her. "Well, you're wrong."

"I'm wrong? Just like that?"

"It's nothing personal," he assured her. "I've heard about Ducky's Bar and it's no place for a lady. I think it's best if I go along for protection."

She stared at him for a long moment. "And I think that's a really bad idea."

"I already told you, I'm fine," he replied without any hesitation. "A blow to the head can't stop Cade Holden."

"Too bad," she muttered behind him as he walked out the front door.

Ducky's Bar sat nestled between Eve's Tattoo Emporium and Barney's Bail Bonds at the far end of Bale Street. Peeling yellow paint adorned the cinder-block wall on the outside of the bar. Black paint concealed the windows and the plate glass door, giving the building an ominous appearance.

The smell of rain hung heavy in the night air and swollen gray clouds stretched across the sky. Cade glanced at Chloe as they walked along the litter-strewn sidewalk. She looked grim, determined, and too damn sexy.

"Hold it," he said, stopping in front of the door. "I've changed my mind. You can't go in there."

She looked up at him. "Excuse me?"

"Go back and wait for me in the truck. I'll check out the place and see if Gino's made an appearance."

Annoyance flashed in her eyes. "I'm not waiting in your truck. I can't believe you'd even suggest such a thing."

"And I can't believe you'd even consider going into a place like Ducky's Bar in that outfit."

She planted her hands on her hips. "You don't like the way I look?"

"You want my honest opinion?" He moved closer to her. "I love the way you look. The problem is that every guy in this bar is going to love it, too. I can't help you find Gino if I'm too busy fighting off all your admirers."

"In the first place," she said, her voice low and tight, "this outfit is called business casual. In the second place, I never asked you to fight anyone. You're barely able to walk, much less defend my honor. And in the third place, it may surprise you to learn that not every man looks at a woman as a sex object."

His jaw tightened. "This has nothing to do with sex and everything to do with that dress you're wearing. He frowned at the way the black dress outlined her figure. "Don't you have a jacket or something you can put on? It's chilly outside."

"I forgot to bring a jacket. I guess I was too distracted by the fact that my brother might be going to prison."

"Then wear mine," he said, reaching into the back of the cab to grab his denim jacket. "It looks like it's about to rain."

She took it from him and reached for the door handle. "Thanks. Now let's quit wasting time and go inside."

They left the pickup truck and headed for the bar.

"Let me do all the talking," Cade said as he walked beside her. "This Ducky woman may be the owner, but I've heard she's a real wacko. She's been married like four or five times."

"That hardly makes her crazy," Chloe said wryly. "Maybe she's just unlucky in love."

"Her husbands were the unlucky ones. They're all dead."

She stopped short. "What are you implying?"

"I'm not implying anything. I'm just telling you that she's a tough lady." He smiled. "But I'm sure I can soften her up. Women find it hard to resist me."

She pushed up the long sleeves of his jacket. "It must be your modesty."

"Must be." Then his smile faded as stared at her. Chloe looked even more sexy wearing his large jacket and Cade was certain he wouldn't be the only man in the bar to notice. "Let's make this quick."

She didn't say anything as he held the door open for her. He followed her inside, taking a moment for his eyes to adjust to the dim lighting and suspicious glances from the bar's patrons. A Willie Nelson tune wailed from the jukebox, accompanied by the shrill bells and whistles of the two pinball machines in the corner.

Cade had only taken three steps inside the bar when a burly bouncer blocked his path.

"I'd like to see some identification," the bouncer said, holding out one beefy hand.

"What about her?" Cade asked, watching as Chloe simply walked past the bouncer unimpeded.

"I'm not here to answer your questions," the bouncer told him.

"You didn't card her, so why single me out? You can't seriously believe I'm under twenty-one."

"Hey, I'm just doing my job," the bouncer said. "If you don't like it, you can jump on your horse and get the hell outta here."

Cade had dealt with plenty of tough guys in his time, but this body-building bouncer had them all beat. He wore his dark hair in a military-style crew cut and tattoos lined both arms. There was a long scar running along his forehead, just above his bushy eyebrows. And his angular nose veered a little to the left.

But despite the throbbing in his head, Cade still thought he could take him. Then he noticed Chloe frowning at him from the bar and realized he didn't have time for this kind of nonsense. "Look, I'm twenty-nine. So quit fooling around and go bother somebody else."

"Why the hell do you keep stalling?" The bouncer's eyes narrowed on him. "Got something to hide? I want to see some ID and I want to see it right now."

Cade could either keep standing there, arguing with this guy, or he could join Chloe at the bar. "Fine," he muttered, reaching into his back pocket for his wallet. Only he came up empty. Both of his back pockets were empty. "Damn."

"Got a problem there, buckaroo?"

Cade definitely had a problem—and his name was Gino. Not only had Chloe's little brother attacked him with his fake dog, but he'd also stolen his wallet. Which meant Cade had no money, no credit cards, and no driver's license.

This just wasn't his day.

Cade cleared his throat, trying to keep one eye on

Chloe. "Would you believe somebody stole my wallet?"

The bouncer snorted. "That's original. I've tossed out boneheaded teenagers with more imagination."

Before Cade could reply, Chloe ambled over to them. "Hey, what's going on here?"

"Please let me handle this," Cade told her, irritated by the bouncer's attitude and the fact that Gino had stolen his wallet.

The bouncer glared at him. "Is that any way to talk to your girlfriend?"

"I'm not his girlfriend," she said quickly.

The bouncer grinned as he turned to Chloe. "Well, that's good to hear. Why don't you let me buy you a beer, girl? Then we can have a private conversation."

Cade stepped in front of Chloe. "Forget it. She's off-limits. Especially to somebody like you."

A muscle ticked in the bouncer's jaw as he took a step closer to them. "Somebody like me?"

"Cade..." Chloe began, moving in front of him.

But this was one time Cade didn't intend to let her interfere. He took a step around her and closed in on the bouncer, one hand curling into a fist. "The woman is with me. If you have a problem with that, we can handle it outside."

The bouncer's grin widened, the light reflecting

off the gold crown on his front tooth. "Sounds good to me. Lead the way."

"Neither one of you are going anywhere!" Chloe exclaimed, stepping between them. Then she glowered up at the bouncer. "What exactly is your problem, Viper?"

"Viper?" Cade echoed, looking from Chloe to the bouncer.

"Meet my cousin," she said, lightly punching the bouncer's arm. "Viper Galetti. Viper, this is Cade Holden."

Viper pointed at Cade. "Chloe, are you really into this guy? Why don't you go for a real man, like my lawyer? That's what I wanted to talk to you about. He told me he'd really like to date you."

Chloe grimaced. "Your lawyer is a slimeball."

"Maybe so," Viper said with a shrug. "But just think how useful it would be to have him in the family. Free legal advice available twenty-four hours a day."

"If you think it's such a great idea, you date him," she retorted. "Besides, I'm not here to talk about my love life. I'm looking for Gino."

"Your brother Gino?"

Chloe rolled her eyes. "How many Ginos do you know?"

Viper shrugged again, avoiding her direct gaze.

"Even if I did see him around, I'm no snitch."

"Then I'll just have to ask Ducky. You told me she knows everything that goes on in this place." Chloe looked around the crowded bar. "Where is she?"

Viper hesitated, his suspicious gaze flicking over Cade. "What about this guy? He claims he doesn't have any ID. How do I know he's not a vice cop disguised as a jerk?"

"If I was a cop, I'd arrest you for dumb-and-disorderly conduct." Then Cade turned to Chloe. "Oh, and about Gino, he took my wallet."

She closed her eyes with a groan. "Oh, Cade, he didn't..."

"He did. Unless the Chihuahua ate it."

Viper flashed his gold tooth. "Sounds like Gino is finally living up to the Galetti name. Now my cousin Chloe here is another story. She's a downright embarrassment to the family. In fact, we used to call her Squeaky, 'cause she's always been so squeaky clean."

Chloe glowered at him, which only seemed to amuse her cousin.

Viper gave a low chuckle. "And because she was always squeaking on all of us, a real tattletale— Ow!" he yelped, his words abruptly cut off as a tiny woman with short, iron-gray hair twisted his ear between her bony fingers.

"That's enough out of you, Virgil Galetti. I've told

you before to stop harassing my customers."

"But Ducky," he protested as she pulled him by the ear toward the bar.

Then Ducky reached over the counter and grabbed a bucket and sponge. "If you don't have anything better to do, you can mop the bathroom floors. I want them shining by the time you're through."

Viper rubbed his red ear. "But Ducky..."

She planted both hands on her hips. "And if I hear one more 'But Ducky,' I'm fixin' to use that sponge to clean out your mouth—*after* you've scrubbed those floors. Now get going."

Cade found himself suddenly approving of the gravelly-voiced, tough-talking dynamo. Even if Ducky did look like a charter member of the Hell's Angels.

Viper paled and backed away, obviously smart enough to take her threat seriously. "Yes, Ducky."

"And don't just barge into the ladies' room without knocking like you did the last time," she admonished as Viper disappeared behind the men's bathroom door.

The little tyrant took a long draw from her e-cigarette, then she turned back to Cade and Chloe. "Welcome to Ducky's Bar."

Chloe smiled up at him. "Cade, I'd like you to meet my grandmother, Ducky Galetti."

5

Chloe bit back a smile at the stunned expression on Cade's face. She probably should have told him sooner, but the man seemed to bring out the worst in her. Especially after he'd practically accused her grandmother of killing off her husbands. Ducky might not be totally legit, but she wasn't dangerous. Or, at least, not lethally dangerous.

Ducky enveloped her granddaughter in an affectionate hug. "It's been too long, my sweet girl. Now, let me take a good look at you." Ducky stepped back and held her at arm's length. "Not bad." She reached out to adjust the bodice of Chloe's dress. "There, that's much better. You know I've always told you there's no reason to hide your best assets."

This time Chloe's smile broke through when she

saw a muscle flex in Cade's cheek. She had to give him credit, though—he exercised surprising restraint.

Ducky turned around and elbowed Cade in the ribs. "Bet you find it hard to believe I'm old enough to be her grandmother."

"Well, I..." His voice trailed off as he looked helplessly at Chloe.

Ducky glanced at her granddaughter. "Is he always this slow or is he just overwhelmed by a double dose of Galetti beauty?"

"You shouldn't be surprised at the effect you have on him, Ducky." Chloe leaned over to kiss her grandmother's wrinkled, rouged cheek. "You've been making men speechless for more than fifty years."

Ducky snorted. "I think it's a shame you never went into the con game, girl. You're one smooth talker."

"Then I should be able to talk you into two ice-cold beers—on the house?"

Ducky cackled. "You've got 'em. Go on and sit at my special table. I'll be right there."

Cade watched her grandmother bustle off toward the bar, a dazed expression on his face. Chloe knew that coping with more than one Galetti at a time tended to have that effect on people. Especially when one of those Galettis was Ducky. She loved her spry, unconventional grandmother, despite her frequent flirtations with the wrong side of the law.

Ducky had been there for Chloe each time her mother had been sent to prison, providing both comfort and advice. Intensely loyal to everyone in the family, Ducky had taken a special interest in her. She'd encouraged her granddaughter's dream to go into interior design and even cosigned her college loan papers. Ducky might not be a typical grandmother, but Chloe loved her fiercely. And that love was returned tenfold.

"She's really your grandmother?" Cade asked as they seated themselves at the secluded table.

Chloe nodded. "Yes, my father's mother. Only she doesn't allow her grandchildren to call her anything but Ducky."

He scowled at her. "You might have told me sooner."

"But, Cade," she said, batting her eyelashes at him, "I thought you already knew everything."

Before he could reply, Ducky arrived at the table with three frosty bottles of beer in her hands. She held Cade's bottle just out of his reach. "I don't serve a drink to a man unless I've had a proper introduction."

He rose to his feet. "I'm Cade Holden," he said, tipping his cowboy hat to her. "Nice to meet you, ma'am."

Chloe leaned forward. "Ducky, we can't stay long."

Ducky waved him back down into his chair, then joined them at the table. "You'll stay long enough for this Holden fella to tell me what his intentions are toward you."

"My intentions are strictly honorable," Cade assured her.

"That's too bad," Ducky said with a sigh. "A man with strictly honorable intentions isn't much fun. Have you even kissed her yet?"

"Ducky!" To Chloe's consternation, a hot blush crept up her neck. "We're not dating; we're just working together—temporarily. And we're not here to talk about kissing. We're here about Gino."

Ducky frowned. "Oh, dear, what's that boy done now?"

"He's in trouble," Chloe replied, glossing over the finer details. "I have to find him. Has he been here this evening?"

Ducky shook her head. "No, but he was here last night. Had some blonde with him, too."

Chloe's eyes widened. "A girl?"

"More like an Amazon," Ducky said with a cackle. "Gino definitely had his hands full."

"Who was she?" Chloe asked.

Ducky shrugged. "Beats me. I was busy in the back room. I just got a glimpse of her."

"What about Cousin Viper," Cade said, "didn't he ask to see her ID?"

"Nope." Ducky tipped up her beer bottle and took a long swig before elaborating. "He was too busy checking out her other vital statistics. She was one of those flashy babes who love to drink and dance on the table. Not that I'm complaining; it's good business for me. But I was afraid Gino might be in over his head."

Chloe glanced at Cade. "I heard he broke up with Nanette, but I didn't realize he was dating someone new."

"I never met that Nanette girl," Ducky said. "But this one was some piece of work. She flirted all night with Virgil. But your brother looked too nervous to notice."

"Poor Gino," Chloe murmured. "He hasn't had much luck with women. No wonder he's been acting a little odd lately."

"How can you tell?" Cade asked.

She ignored him. "Is there anything else I should know?"

Ducky set her beer bottle on the table. "I shouldn't have told you that much. It's time to let him go, Chloe. Gino is a grown man now and he doesn't need you to look after him anymore."

Chloe blinked, surprised by the vehemence in her grandmother's voice. "But he's family."

"Of course, he's family. He'll always be family. But there's more to life than work and cleaning up Gino's messes. Just look at you." Ducky's mouth drew down in a frown. "You're out on the town with this mouthwatering hunk of man and you're wasting it by worrying about your little brother."

Her words pricked. She'd always been proud of taking care of Gino. How could she just look the other way if her brother was headed for trouble? How could she not lift a finger to stop it?

"If you want to know the truth," Chloe said slowly, "Cade believes Gino bashed him in the head this evening when he came to see me."

"Impossible," Ducky said, without a flicker of her false eyelashes. "That isn't Gino's style. He's not a violent person."

"He almost cut off my toe the other day," Cade told her. "And tonight, he answered the door with a butcher knife in his hand."

"Sorry, I don't buy it," Ducky said, staring him down. "The sight of blood makes Gino hysterical. You must be mistaken, Mr. Holden."

"I have the stitches on my toe to prove it," Cade insisted. "But that's not all. We found a bag full of—"

"Potato chips," Chloe interjected, before Cade could spill the beans about the diamonds. "They were lying on the kitchen floor and Gino had disappeared. I thought maybe something had happened to him."

Even though she had lied through most of her childhood, she still wasn't very good at it, which was evident by the way Cade and Ducky were gaping at her. But it was too late to backpedal now. "You know how Gino loves potato chips. He wouldn't leave a bag just lying around, especially on the floor. But maybe I am overreacting just a bit." She pushed her chair back and stood up. "Ready to go, Cade?"

He looked at the untouched beer in front of him. "Uh... sure."

"Bye, Ducky." She leaned over and kissed her grandmother's cheek. "Be good."

"I'll be good if you'll be a little bit bad," Ducky replied. Then she turned to Cade, her brown eyes serious. "I want you to promise me that you'll take good care of my granddaughter."

"Ducky..." Chloe began.

"Promise me," Ducky said, her voice more intense now and her bony fingers tightly squeezing his forearm.

He winced. "I promise."

Ducky's shoulders relaxed. "Thank you." Then she turned to Chloe. "I like him. I think you should keep this one."

"Ducky, like I told you before, we're not dating." Truth be told, Chloe was surprised Cade Holden had stuck around this long. It was highly doubtful he'd come back for more. Then she smiled at her grandmother. "Besides, when we first met, he told me he had no interest in sleeping with me."

"You know that was a misunderstanding," he protested.

"So, you *do* want to sleep with my granddaughter?" Ducky asked him.

Cade looked between the two women, panic flaring in his blue eyes. "Well, um... no... we're just business partners."

Ducky laughed. "And I thought Chloe was a bad liar. Looks like you two are made for each other."

"His grandmother thinks so." Chloe kissed Ducky's cheek, then turned on her heel and walked to his pickup truck. Cade waved to Ducky before following her. A gentle rain had fallen while they were inside the bar, making the pavement glisten under the streetlights.

He waited until they were a safe distance from Ducky's Bar before asking the obvious question. "What was that all about?"

Chloe sat silently in the passenger seat, staring at her cell phone. She looked up at Cade. "What?"

"That crazy potato chip story you told your grandmother. I think it's obvious she didn't buy it."

"Oh, I know. But I didn't want Ducky to find out about the diamonds."

"Are you afraid she'd want them for herself?" he asked wryly.

"Yes."

Cade almost missed his corner. He maneuvered the turn, then glanced over at her. "You're joking, right?"

"Unfortunately, no." She didn't say anything for a long moment. "Look, the Galettis aren't exactly like other families."

That was the understatement of the year. Cade had never met anyone like Chloe. He never wanted to meet anyone like her grandmother. Especially in a deserted alley. His forearm and ribs still hurt.

Light raindrops fell from the sky and splattered against the windshield. Cade turned on the wipers. "You really think she'd take the diamonds from you?"

"Yes, to protect me," Chloe replied. "But then she'd probably sell them on the black market. Ducky has cleaned up her act over the years, but she still runs a high-stakes poker game in the back room of her bar. It's in her blood. A bag of diamonds might prove irresistible to her."

"It's in her blood, but not in yours?"

Chloe smiled. "That's right. I must have some kind of genetic mutation."

"Lucky for you," he said and meant it. The rain grew heavier, obscuring his vision, so he turned the wipers to the highest setting. "Exactly how long has this crime gene been in your family?"

She leaned her head back against the headrest. "I believe it started with my great-great- grandfather. He was a professional gambler who got shot in the back after he was accused of cheating. Over the years, that story's been romanticized by making him some kind of rogue hero. Gino was even named after him."

"Was he a card cheat?"

She shrugged. "Who knows? All that matters to me is making sure the current Gino Galetti isn't accused of any illegal activities."

Cade glanced over at her. "But we already know he stole the diamonds."

"He may be the prime suspect," she said, her fingers fidgeting with the gold clasp of her purse. "But we still don't know for certain. And he's not answering any of my texts." She dropped the cell phone into her purse. "Look, even if Gino did steal them, there's no reason he can't put them back where they belong."

Cade pulled up in front of her house, cut the engine, then turned to look at her. "That wasn't part of our agreement."

But Chloe wasn't looking at him. Her gaze was fixed on the front door. The *open* front door. "Didn't I lock the door when we left?"

"I watched you lock it. Which means—"

"Which means," she interjected, her expression grim as she popped open the passenger door, "it's time to settle this once and for all."

Cade jumped out of the pickup truck and hastily followed right on her heels, rain pelting him. His sore head pounded with each step, but he didn't want her confronting Gino alone. If the guy was desperate, there was no telling what he might do—even to his own sister.

Chloe stopped abruptly in the open doorway to take off the damp denim jacket and Cade plowed into her. He grabbed her shoulders to keep her from falling, then almost fell over himself when he looked past her into the house.

It was a disaster.

His fingers flexed on her shoulders as he surveyed the house. Furniture lay upended on the floor, the upholstery ripped to shreds and the white stuffing pulled out and scattered over the floor. The twenty-seven-inch television set had been tipped on its side and the back panel removed, the picture tube and electrical components exposed. Fortunately, it looked as if the antique windows and beautiful woodwork hadn't been touched.

Chloe leaned back against him for a moment, almost as if she couldn't support herself. He breathed in the subtle vanilla scent of her hair and his gaze fell on her slender neck, now so close to his lips. They tingled slightly as he imagined skimming light, caressing kisses over that soft, creamy skin.

But the fantasy abruptly ended when Chloe straightened and strode further into her living room. She turned in a slow circle as she took in the devastation.

Cade took a deep breath to collect himself, then followed her inside. "What the hell happened here?"

"Isn't it obvious?" she muttered before disappearing down the long hallway.

He followed her wordlessly as she surveyed the rest of the house, both upstairs and down. Each room had been searched by the vandal, with no care given to the mess left behind. But just like the first floor, none of the unique windows, carved moldings, or antique fixtures had been damaged on the upper floors.

Which told Cade this was an inside job.

Chloe saved Gino's bedroom for last. Squaring her shoulders, she opened the door. Then she let out a gasp.

Cade moved up close behind her and silently shook his head. It was the worst room of all. The closet stood empty, the clothes flung haphazardly over the floor. The dresser had been upended, the wood panels on the back and bottom pried off. The mattress lay at a drunken angle on the bed, slashed open through the blue-striped sheet and all the way through to the other side.

Chloe bent down to pick up a small ragged clown doll off the floor. Time had faded its curly red hair and orange polka-dot jumpsuit, but the jagged tear from nose to navel looked brand new.

"Our dad gave this to Gino when he was ten years old," she said, her voice void of emotion. "It had belonged to my father when he was a little boy and Gino had wanted it so badly. He promised he'd never let anything happen to it."

Cade carefully took the clown from her hand and set it on the tilted mattress. Then he enfolded Chloe in his arms. He gently cupped the back of her head with his hand, burying her face in the crook of his shoulder. "Go ahead and cry."

Her head snapped up, her brown eyes blazing.

"Cry? I'd rather kick something. Or rather, someone! How dare they destroy my house just because they couldn't get their greedy hands on those diamonds."

A clap of thunder sounded above them, so close it shook the house.

"How do you know they didn't?" Cade asked, realizing he hadn't yet checked underneath the stairs.

"Because I've had them with me all evening." She held up her purse. "Safe and sound."

His jaw sagged. Thousands of dollars' worth of diamonds had been in her purse this whole time, in his car, and in Ducky's Bar. And he hadn't known it. A hundred possible scenarios popped in his head, all of them bad. "Are you completely crazy?"

"I'd call it prudent." She glanced around the room. "Especially considering what happened here."

"What if the police had made a traffic stop and searched your purse?"

"For what? A piece of chewing gum?"

"For any number of reasons," he said, now pacing back and forth across the floor. "Or what if we'd been in a car accident and some emergency room nurse had found them? Or some guy had decided to mug you outside of Ducky's Bar?"

"I had you for protection."

"You might have mentioned to me that you also brought a stash of hot diamonds along for the ride."

She stared up at him. "Why are you so upset about this? I'm the one who deserves to be upset. My house has just been ransacked."

"Thanks to your brother."

Her brown eyes widened. "You think Gino did this?"

"Oh, please. Don't tell me you're still going to keep defending him." Cade pointed to the doll. "He just killed a clown!"

"How many times do I have to tell you," she said, her voice growing weary now. "This is not Gino's style."

Cade shoved the mattress back into position on the bed, then sat down, pulling her down beside him. "I think it's time you faced some facts, Chloe. It looks like Gino is on some sort of crazy crime spree."

She turned to face him. "Accidentally nicking you with a power saw does not make him public enemy number one."

"It was more than a nick," he countered, stung by her sarcasm. "But I don't even care about that anymore. He's become much more dangerous in the past few hours." Cade let his gaze wander around the room. The destruction had a malevolent air about it. "You're not staying here tonight."

She blinked at him. "Is that an order?"

"Yes. And it isn't up for debate. It's not safe here. Can you stay with Ducky?"

"Of course. But I have no intention of going anywhere."

Cade couldn't contain his frustration. "Chloe, please be sensible."

She rolled her eyes. "I like you so much better when you don't open your mouth."

"That's funny," he replied, "I was just thinking the same thing about you." *Except when you kiss me*. He looked away from her mouth and stared hard at the floor.

Why did this woman have to make everything so difficult? Why did she have to have a face like an angel and a hot body that burned away his brain cells? Why couldn't he just walk away?

"I'm guessing your idea of the perfect woman is one who is quiet and meek," Chloe told him, "but I'm not built that way."

"Believe me," Cade muttered, "I'm not complaining about the way you're built."

Her cheeks flushed a becoming pink. "Well, if you'd pay as much attention to my brain, maybe we could actually accomplish something."

"I happen to think you're a very intelligent woman," he said honestly. "Except where your brother is concerned. Even you have to admit you're more than a little biased."

"Maybe so. But like I said before, I know Gino better than anyone. He may have stolen those diamonds, but he didn't do this." Her hand swept around the chaotic room.

"Then who did? Some other Galetti?"

She slowly shook her head. "Not unless it was Uncle Alfred. He's not technically my uncle anymore since Aunt Mary divorced him. None of the family has had anything to do with him since his arrest for pandering. Even the Galettis know where to draw the line."

"So, you think Uncle Alfred is responsible?"

"I don't know what to think." She rubbed her face with her hands. "It's even possible this mess has nothing to do with the diamonds. Maybe this is just a run-of-the-mill burglary."

"Maybe," he conceded. "Have you noticed anything missing?"

"Just my brother."

"So much for that theory."

"Do you have a better one?" She tipped up her chin. "Besides blaming Gino?"

"It's still the most logical explanation," he insisted. "But have you considered he could have an accomplice? Or even more than one?"

"No." She frowned. "Actually, the thought never even crossed my mind. Gino doesn't have a lot of friends."

"They wouldn't necessarily have to be friends. What about the blonde that Ducky mentioned?"

"I suppose it's possible," she conceded, her expression growing thoughtful.

"I'd say it's highly likely. Which means we definitely have to call the police."

She turned to him. "But..."

"No buts," he said, steeling himself against her entreaties. "We've taken enough risks tonight already. I still can't believe you brought those diamonds along with us."

"That again?" One corner of her mouth twisted in exasperation. "Even if by some wild chance the police did discover them in our possession, all we'd have to do is explain the situation. They'd have no reason to suspect either one of us."

"Unless one of us is a convicted felon."

"I'm not!" she said hotly.

"I am."

Chloe gaped at him in disbelief. Then she closed her mouth and tried to pretend his admission hadn't just knocked the air out of her lungs. Why should it shock her so much? It wasn't as if she'd never met a convicted felon before. And not just one. Over half the Galetti family had done time at one point or another.

But Cade Holden?

"You don't believe me?" he said, a half smile tugging at his mouth.

"Frankly... no," she said at last. "You're just not the type."

"Should I take that as a compliment?"

"Of course." She frowned at him, still confused by his confession. "What happened? Were you framed?"

He shook his head. "Nope. I was stone-cold guilty. Some no-account friends and I celebrated my twenty-first birthday by breaking into a horse stable. Then we took some prize-winning Arabian show horses out for a midnight ride."

"Well," she said slowly, "that's not the worst crime I've ever heard. The horses weren't hurt, were they?"

"No, by pure dumb luck, the police caught us before we could get too far on them. That's when we learned each one of those horses was worth more than one hundred thousand dollars."

"Oh, no," Chloe breathed. "That makes it a felony."

"Yep," he replied. "And to make matters worse, I

had an extensive record. Street fighting, drag racing, disturbing the peace—in other words, a hellraiser."

Her gaze drifted to his mouth as he spoke. She'd kissed him tonight. Twice. Even worse, she'd enjoyed kissing him. "Why didn't you tell me sooner?"

"That I was a cowboy outlaw? It's not exactly something I'm proud of, Chloe. I messed up. Big-time. But I'm not that same man anymore. I've turned my life around and I have Grandma Hattie to thank for it."

"What did she do?"

"She convinced the judge to give me the minimum sentence. Which included three years of community service after I got out of jail. She also told me in no uncertain terms that my parents weren't ever coming back."

Chloe blinked. "That sounds a bit harsh."

He nodded, a muscle knotting his jaw. "True. But I needed to hear it."

"Why? That seems so cruel."

Cade was silent for so long she thought he wasn't going to answer her.

"I was so bitter about losing them," he said at last. "And so angry. Like I told you, I was only five years old when the car accident happened. And as I grew up, I couldn't..." Cade's voice broke, then he continued. "I couldn't remember them."

Chloe moved closer to him. "And you decided life wasn't fair?"

He looked up at her and nodded. "And if life wasn't fair, I figured I didn't have to follow the rules either. Truth be told, I was a handful for my grandparents growing up. I had a real talent for finding trouble."

"You probably just wanted attention," she said, remembering how Gino had always caused the most trouble when their parents weren't there for him.

"That's right, I guess, but I sure went about it all wrong." He met her gaze. "Then after the horse theft, Grandma Hattie asked me if I wanted to dishonor my parents' memory by continuing to break the law, or if I wanted to honor them by being the best man I could be. That being a good man was a gift I could give to them." He cleared his throat. "The only gift I'd ever be able to give to them."

"That's beautiful," she said softly.

"It's what I needed to hear." Cade smiled, the tension leaving his body. "I still wonder how Grandma Hattie kept her patience with my wild ways —and kept herself from throwing me through a window."

"I can see why she'd be tempted," Chloe teased.

"I guess she loved me enough to tell me the hard truth—my parents were never coming back, and I could either make something of my life or destroy it. But whichever I chose, I knew she'd always be there for me."

Chloe's throat tightened at his words. At the image of a little boy who missed his parents so desperately. Anger roiled inside Chloe until she wanted to punch something. Why did his story affect her so much? It was very sad, but she didn't know his parents. She barely knew Cade.

Then it hit her.

In their own way, Chloe's parents had abandoned her and Gino when they were children. They hadn't died, but with every crime they'd committed, they'd risked breaking up the family.

Without conscious thought, she reached out and clasped Cade's large hand, squeezing it gently. No wonder she'd felt that odd connection between them. They shared more than passion. They shared heartache and loss.

She gazed up into his sapphire-blue eyes as her anger transformed itself into something else entirely. Her heart pounded in her chest and her breath quickened. She let her hand trail over his wrist and up his arm, so lightly she barely touched him. His body stilled and she heard his quick intake of breath as her fingers traced his shoulder and the strong column of his neck, slowly circling the top button of his collar.

"Chloe," he groaned, but not making a move to stop her.

She didn't say anything, just kept touching him. His long, lean jaw, his cheek, and the line of his brow, carefully avoiding the wound on his temple. Then her fingers drifted into his thick dark hair, brushing through it until she reached the crisp, tight curls at the nape of his neck.

He reached out to cup her cheek, taking his turn to touch and torment. His broad fingers outlined her cheekbone and the delicate shell of her ear. Then he lightly trailed the tips of his fingers down her neck, the sensation causing an odd warmth to spread throughout her body. Then he replaced his fingertips with his lips, lightly kissing the length of her neck with agonizing slowness.

A hot blush suffused her cheeks, and she closed her eyes, amazed that such delicate kisses could have such a devastating effect on her.

The ringing of her cell phone on the nightstand made them both jump. Cade's mouth stilled on the crook of her neck. Then he sat up and they stared at each other for a long moment as her cell phone continued to ring.

"I'd better answer it," she whispered. Struggling to compose herself, she picked up the phone and saw the word PRIVATE on the screen. Her skin still tingled everywhere Cade had touched her. She took a deep breath as she answered the call. "Hello?"

Her eyes widened when she heard the voice on the other end of the line. Then she looked at Cade and mouthed the words, "It's Gino."

6

Cade watched Chloe pace, twisting a lock of hair between her fingers. Judging from her stark silence, Gino was doing all the talking.

He ran one finger around the collar of his shirt, unsettled by what had almost happened here. Being attracted to Chloe Galetti was one thing. Acting on that attraction was quite another.

"Listen, Gino..." Her voice trailed off as she looked at Cade in frustration.

Cade was frustrated, too. This business meeting wasn't turning out at all the way he'd planned. Even worse, there was nothing fake about his reaction to her. His fingers itched to touch her again. He wanted to hold her. Kiss her.

"You can't be serious," she said, her fingers tightening on the cell phone. "Gino—"

Cade watched Chloe's lips press firmly together as her brother obviously cut her off again. Those delectable lips had attempted to breathe life into him earlier this evening.

And it had worked.

These past few hours with Chloe had been more intense, more exhilarating, more unpredictable than anything he could ever remember experiencing. She was like no woman he'd ever met before. And she was completely wrong for him.

She was a Galetti, he reminded himself. Strike one. She was Gino's sister. Strike two. She made him completely crazy. Strike three. He didn't want craziness in his life. He'd had enough of that during his outlaw years.

Now he just wanted to get his life back under control.

"Gino, please," she entreated into the phone.

He moved toward Chloe. "Hey, let me try to talk to him."

She shook her head and turned away from him. "All right, I'm listening..."

Time to take matters into his own hands.

He reached for the cell phone, pulling it gently but firmly out of her grasp. Then he held it up to his ear. "Gino, this is Cade."

Chloe glared at him, but he ignored her. She was

obviously too emotionally involved to handle this on her own.

"What the hell are you still doing there with my sister?" Gino sputtered. "No, don't tell me. I don't want to know. Whatever it is, you'd better stop it right now. I mean it, Holden, if you lay one finger on Chloe—"

"It's time to stop playing games, Gino. *We* know you're guilty and *you* know you're guilty. Now why don't you buck up and take responsibility? It's time to turn yourself over to the police. The longer you wait, the harder it's going to be on you."

Gino replied by abruptly ending the call.

Cade stared at the cell phone for a moment, then handed it to Chloe. "He hung up on me."

"There's a shocker."

He blinked at her tone. "Why the sarcasm? He's your brother."

"Because I'm mad." She slammed the cell phone down on the bed. "No, not just mad. I'm furious."

"Gino does have that effect on people."

"Gino?" She gaped at him in disbelief. "What about you?"

"Me?" For a moment, he wondered if she was taking her anger and frustration at Gino out on him. She certainly wasn't making much sense. "What did I do?"

"Well, for starters, you took the phone right out of my hand. Then you probably scared Gino out of his wits by bringing up the police and telling him he should turn himself in."

"I'm sorry for taking your phone," he said. "I just wanted to help, but I can be a little bullheaded sometimes. And from the sound of it, you weren't getting anywhere with him."

"I was *listening* to him." She sat down on the side of the bed. "You should try it sometime, instead of barging in where you're not wanted."

"Hey, I listen," he replied, stung by her words. Not wanted? She'd wanted him a few moments ago, before Gino had interfered with that phone call. Or had she? Maybe Cade had just assumed the explosive reaction between them was mutual. Maybe this attraction had only been real for him. "Look, I know I was out of line. It's been a long, crazy evening and I'm sure we're both tired."

"And you did take a blow to the head, so I shouldn't have snapped at you." She rose to her feet. "You're right, Cade, it has been a long evening. I think you should go home now and get some rest."

"Don't you want me to wait until the police arrive?"

She blanched. "The police?"

He motioned at the chaos around them. "You have to report this."

"Says who?"

He took a deep, calming breath, refusing to let himself lose his temper. "I'm not trying to tell you what to do. It's your house, your brother, your mess. But any reasonable person..."

"Any reasonable person," she interjected, "would realize that Gino won't come within a mile of this house if there are police cruisers parked outside. Besides, it doesn't look like anything's been stolen. Whoever did this was on a search-and-destroy mission."

"Searching for the diamonds," he added. "Which means they could come back here at any time." He set his jaw. "You can't stay here alone, Chloe."

"Cade..." she warned.

"What I mean," he interjected, mentally kicking himself, "is that I'd rather you didn't stay here alone. If you don't want to leave, then I'll sleep here."

"No," she said a little too quickly. "That's not necessary. You've already done too much."

Cade hadn't done what he'd really wanted to do. Which worried him almost as much as the thought of her staying in the house by herself. His willpower was strong, but not superhuman.

"I'll call Viper," she offered at last. "I'm sure he won't mind camping out on the sofa."

"Fine." Cade knew he should feel relieved instead of frustrated. He'd finally won an argument. Instead, his concern deepened as he reluctantly followed Chloe out of the bedroom and down the grand staircase to the front door.

She walked out onto the porch with him. "Good night, Cade. This is one night I'll never forget."

"Me either," he muttered, still feeling uneasy about leaving her. "Lock all your doors and windows."

She gave him a mock salute. "Yes, sir."

He grinned in spite of himself. "All right. So maybe I do tend to come on a little strong sometimes. I'll try to work on it."

She smiled, the moonlight casting an ethereal glow on her face. "Don't try too hard, cowboy. Some women like that in a man."

"But not you?"

A light breeze fluttered the hem of her dress around her slender legs. "I guess I've been on my own too long to start taking orders now. But we're professionals, so I'm sure we can still work together."

"Definitely." He took a step closer to her. "Will I see you tomorrow?"

She nodded, her eyes large and luminous as she

looked up at him. "I'll be at the café site after lunch. I need to measure the windows."

"I'll be there, too," he promised, resisting the urge to brush back the silky hair on her temple. It was even harder to resist kissing her good night. But he'd had all the temptation he could take for one evening. So, he just stood there, watching her, the air crackling between them.

At last Chloe moved back to the door. "Good night, Cade."

"Good night." He headed down the wooden steps, then he turned abruptly. "Wait a minute."

She paused in the open doorway. "What?"

"You never told me about your phone conversation with Gino. Did he tell you where he was?"

"No."

"Well, did he happen to say when he was coming back? Or where he got the diamonds? Or why he left me under the staircase?"

She took a step back into the house, the vintage screen door closing between them. "I didn't get a chance to ask him. He was sort of rambling."

Cade climbed back onto the porch and pulled the screen door open. "About what?"

"This and that. I'm so tired now I can't even think straight. I'll tell you all about it tomorrow." She reached for the front door handle.

"Chloe, wait…"

But he was too late. The door swung closed, and Chloe disappeared inside, locking it after her.

He swore softly under his breath, certain she was keeping something from him. Part of him wanted to bang on the oak door, demanding answers. Unfortunately, that was the part of him she didn't like. He clenched his jaw, wondering what the hell he should do now. He could leave and hope she followed through on her intention to call Viper. Or he could park his pickup truck on the corner and watch over her himself.

His stomach growled as he made his way to the pickup truck. With any luck, he'd have some licorice in his glove compartment for a midnight snack.

It was going to be a very long night.

The next day, Cade couldn't stop looking at his watch. He brushed fine sawdust off the crystal and swore softly under his breath. Two o'clock. He'd been working at the café for hours. Where the hell was Chloe?

He considered himself a patient man. That was a necessity for both his life as a rancher and his side job as a contractor. Each occupation required precision and perseverance. Whether he was working cattle or building a house, hurrying through either job could cost him both time and money. He brought that same studied patience to his personal life, too.

Like his perfect-wife project.

His search might be slow and boring, but he believed his method meant a happily-ever-after outcome was practically guaranteed. No whirlwind romances for Cade Holden. No headlong rush into marriage without looking at the future from every conceivable angle.

But even a patient man can be pushed too far. Especially a man who had just spent a sleepless night cuddled up to a steering wheel. His neck still ached from reclining in the driver's seat of his pickup truck for several hours. At least he hadn't seen anyone trying to sneak into Chloe's house. Even better, she hadn't seen him keeping watch.

She also hadn't called her cousin Viper to stay with her, which only added to his irritation. Maybe she didn't plan to show up here today, either. He should have demanded answers from her last night when he had the chance. Instead, he'd let her practically push him out the front door without explaining anything about Gino's phone call. The phone call that had come just in the nick of time.

He closed his eyes, remembering those heated

moments before her cell phone had jolted them back to reality. Her skin like silk beneath his fingertips. The unsteady rise and fall of her chest. Her lips slightly parted, so lush and inviting. He swallowed hard and opened his eyes. Maybe it was a good thing she had pushed him out the door, or they might still be on that bed.

He couldn't afford to take any more chances. It was bad enough that this mess with Chloe was going to delay his search for a wife. Bad enough that he couldn't work up any enthusiasm to start dating again. Bad enough that he still hadn't called the police about those hot diamonds.

The memory of her voice teased his senses. *I'll be at the café site after lunch.* He set down the plywood on the sawhorse with a bang. It was now two hours past noon and Chloe was nowhere in sight.

If he was smart, he'd want her to stay that way. Only he couldn't seem to concentrate on anything else. He'd re-measured the chair railing three times already. Broke the blade on his jigsaw. And stubbed his sore toe against a four-by-four post.

The oilcloth curtain separating the newly reno-vated kitchen from the dining room of the café suddenly swept open, blowing his blueprints off the makeshift table and onto the floor. Chloe walked in like a gust of fresh air, her brown eyes sparkling and a becoming flush on her cheeks.

"Sorry I'm late," she said, slightly breathless. "I had lunch at Julio's. They have the best Mexican food in town."

"They sure do," he agreed.

She took off her sunglasses but avoided his gaze. It was almost as if last night had never happened. "And then, I was stalled by a cattle drive across the highway. I was stuck there for a good thirty minutes before the road was clear. I hope I didn't keep you waiting."

"No problem," he said in a clipped voice, watching her pull a sketch pad out of her voluminous straw tote bag.

Chloe put her sunglasses in her bag, then looked around the kitchen. "Shall we start in the dining room? That's where most of my designs come into play."

"Sure." He pulled the oilcloth back for her. "Lead the way."

Cade grabbed his blueprints and followed her into the dining room. "Carly and Jack might stop by later this afternoon. I'd like to get our top designs in front of them so they can choose which direction they want to go."

"Good, I'm looking forward to meeting them."

Chloe set her bag on the nearest table. "And I've brought all my sketches with me, along with some sample paints, fabrics, and decorative tiles." Then she took a moment to look around the café, turning in a slow circle. "Wow, Hattie showed me around this place on the day she hired me, but I had no idea it could be transformed into something like this."

"Thanks," he said with a grin. "I like it when people underestimate me."

"I have to admit, I'm impressed. I love that you added the exposed brick and the wooden ceiling beams. And I thought this original plank flooring was a lost cause, but somehow you've managed to bring it back to life."

He felt a warm glow inside. "I'm glad you like it."

"It's fantastic," she told him, her eyes wide with appreciation. "You're very talented at this, Cade, and I can't believe how much progress you've made in such a short time."

"And now that Gino's no longer here to assist me, my progress should be even faster." As soon as he said the words, he wanted to take them back.

Her eyes narrowed. "You're unbelievable," she breathed. "My brother may not be as talented as you. Or as tall and handsome. He may not have sapphire eyes that make a woman's knees go weak, but that doesn't mean he's a loser."

"I never called him a loser," Cade shot back, feeling off-balance. Had she just complimented him or chastised him? "Honestly, Chloe, your brother is a lousy carpenter's apprentice, although he appears to be a pretty good jewel thief. That's not a promising career plan, but maybe you're the one who doesn't give him enough credit. Maybe he could turn those skills into a legitimate career if he quit looking for trouble."

She flinched at his words but didn't back down. "Now it sounds like you're defending him. Last night you wanted to turn Gino over to the police."

"I still do." He rubbed one hand over his jaw, trying to make her understand. "It's for his own good, Chloe. I know that better than anyone. Gino might get hurt or worse if there's a manhunt out for him."

"Don't even say that." She sucked in a deep breath. "Maybe I am overprotective. Maybe that's been my mistake all along."

His mistake was looking into her big brown eyes. They did strange things to his equilibrium. His knees felt like they were made of straw. He forced his gaze away, perplexed by the effect she had on him. "It's obvious we need to talk about this."

"We do, but now isn't the time or the place." She took a deep breath. "I'm sorry I got us off topic. We have a job to do here, and I can't let Gino's predicament or anything else keep me from giving my all for my client." She smoothed one hand over the hostess station he'd built with reclaimed barn wood. "Just like you do."

He admired her dedication, but also sensed how important it was for Chloe to make a name for herself in the interior design business. Gino would have to wait.

"Okay," Cade agreed. "Let's get started."

For the next two hours, they pored over her design plans, discussing ideas and comparing them to his blueprints. Within the first five minutes, he realized Chloe had a true passion for her work. Within the first ten minutes, he found himself engaged in a spirited back-and-forth of ambient lighting versus task lighting—a subject which had never interested him before. The rest of the time, they brainstormed new ideas in rapid succession.

"Wow," she said at last, her cheeks lightly flushed. "We've finally narrowed it down to the top three design plans and I've got them ready to go in a portfolio. You can give it to Carly the next time you see her, then she can choose which plan she wants for her café."

"What if she wants a few elements from each design?"

Chloe smiled. "I can work with that. In fact, I like

it when clients want to add their own special touches to the project. It can be a challenge, but that's part of the fun."

That's when Cade realized the past two hours had been more fun than work. Probably because neither one of them had mentioned the stolen diamonds or her missing brother. She'd asked for time last night and he'd given it to her, but the clock was ticking. And the longer he kept quiet about Gino's crime, the greater the danger that he'd be implicated too.

With his record, Cade simply couldn't take that risk.

"It's time to talk about Gino," he began. "I'd like to know what he told you last night—word for word."

She placed her sketchbooks and samples back in her bag. "I'm a professional, Cade. I don't discuss personal matters during business hours."

"You're stalling again."

She slung the tote bag over her shoulder. "Maybe I should come back when you're in a better mood."

"You're not going anywhere until you tell me what I want to know." He picked up a folded newspaper from a nearby table and thrust it at her. "Did you see the article on the front page of the *Pine City Herald* this morning? The headline is: *Diamond Heist at Akana Jewelers. Suspect Still at Large.*"

Chloe glanced at the paper in front of her, then pushed it aside. "I'm not doing this now, Cade."

"If your brother turns himself in, he may be able to cop a plea. Where is he, Chloe?"

She handed him one of her business cards. "Will you please give this to Carly and have her call me at her earliest convenience?"

Cade rounded the table to stand in front of her. He'd reached the end of his patience. "Come on, Chloe. I deserve to know the truth."

The door to the café opened, heralding a new arrival, but neither one bothered to look. They were completely focused on each other.

Her eyes flashed. "The truth? The truth is that I don't take orders from anyone, Cade. Especially not a stubborn cowboy like you. So, you can take your orders and shove 'em in your... cowboy boot."

"There's no room in my boot, thanks to your brother. My toe is still swollen."

"Don't worry," she retorted, "it's still not as big as your head."

His gaze fell to her mouth. *Damn.* The woman drove him crazy. Unfortunately, he could think of only one way to change the conversation.

But before he could make a move, Chloe muttered under her breath, "Looks like we have an audience."

Cade glanced over his shoulder to see Carly and Jack watching them from the front of the café. He turned back to Chloe. "It's my brother and his fiancée. They can wait until we settle this."

"It's settled," she insisted. "Gino is my problem, not yours. I'll handle it. Just pretend it never happened. Even better, pretend we never even met."

"We're supposed to be working together," he reminded her. "That's part of our deal, remember?"

"We just did. I think we can each handle the rest of the project on our own. In fact, the sooner Hattie realizes we're not a good match, the sooner she can find you a woman who meets all your requirements."

Cade feared that he'd pushed her too far. He moved close to her, knowing some people found his height and size intimidating, but too frustrated to care. "What if I'm not ready to let you go?"

"Then you need to get ready," she whispered, pushing past him and heading toward the door.

Cade watched her leave, barely resisting the urge to race after her. Maybe this was for the best. He might be attracted to her, but there was certainly no future for them. And he could hardly barge back into her life when she'd just made it clear she wanted him out of it.

"Earth to Cade," Jack said, waving a hand in front of his brother's face.

Cade blinked, then realized Jack and Carly were now standing in front of him. "What?"

"So that's Chloe," Carly said, a dimple flashing in one cheek. "I like her."

Jack laughed. "I think Cade likes her too."

Cade rolled up his blueprints, trying to steady his racing heart. "You don't know what you're talking about."

"You seem upset," Carly said, elbowing her fiancé in the ribs. "Do you want to tell us about it?"

"I'm not upset." Cade stuffed the blueprints back into their cylindrical case. "Why should I be upset?"

Jack shrugged. "Maybe because you just let a beautiful woman walk out the door."

"Let her? How was I supposed to stop her? More to the point, why should I stop her? She's a Galetti. I should be celebrating."

"You don't look very happy about it," Jack observed.

"I'm ecstatic," Cade snarled. "In fact, let's celebrate down at the Wildcat Tavern. I'm buying."

"Now?" Jack glanced at his watch.

"Right now," Cade insisted as he moved toward the door. "You can toast my success because I just made a lucky escape from one of Grandma Hattie's matchmaking traps."

Chloe sat in a dark corner booth at the Wildcat Tavern, staring gloomily into her coffee. It was strong and black and a little bitter. Nothing like Hattie Holden's special blackberry cordial. Just the way no other man was quite like Cade Holden.

She watched him through her lashes as he talked and joked with Jack, Carly, and two other handsome cowboys at a table on the far side of the room. They hadn't seen her when they'd entered the Wildcat Tavern and she intended to keep it that way. She'd already walked away from Cade once. She wasn't sure she could do it again.

Keeping Cade in the dark was the only way to keep him safe. She certainly couldn't tell him about Gino's phone call. Her nitwit brother had offered to split the diamonds with her, fifty-fifty. Even worse, Gino believed she would consider the idea. Right now, all she was considering was locking her twenty-two-year-old brother in his room until he came to his senses.

She took a sip of her coffee, grimacing at the bitter taste. It matched the bitterness in her heart. Until last night, she'd truly believed that Gino was innocent. That somehow, he hadn't been behind the theft of those diamonds. But his phone call had made his guilt perfectly clear. He knew about the diamonds. Knew they'd been taken from the hiding place under the stairway.

And now he wanted them back.

Too bad. She set down her coffee cup so hard it clinked against the saucer. She glanced up, then breathed a sigh of relief that no one at Cade's table had noticed. They were too caught up in their conversation. For a moment, she envied their easy camaraderie. The Galettis were loyal and loving, but there had always been an underlying tension among them. Hardly surprising when half of them were wanted by the law at any given time.

She'd just never imagined her brother would be one of them. Until last night. She'd played along with Gino on that phone call, pretending to consider his offer to split the diamonds between them. That's when he'd suggested they meet Sunday night at nine o'clock sharp, by the Dairy Wizard, an abandoned ice cream parlor out on Farmington Road.

Chloe wasn't exactly sure what she'd do when she got there. Gino had sounded different on the phone —almost desperate. She doubted he'd listen to reason. Which meant she had to come up with a plan.

She glanced at the time on her cell phone and realized she couldn't waste another moment feeling sorry for herself. After placing a generous tip on the table, she eased out the back entrance, certain Cade hadn't spotted her. It was already past five o'clock. Somehow in the next twenty-four hours, she had to figure out a way to clear her brother, get rid of the diamonds, and forget about Cade Holden.

Right now, all three sounded impossible.

7

On Sunday evening, Cade walked out of his house and headed toward the barn. He didn't know what to do with himself, especially since he'd already checked cattle, finished the evening chores, and eaten all the cold leftovers in the fridge for supper.

Most Sunday nights like this, he'd be stretched out on the sofa, watching a football game. But he just couldn't seem to focus. It had been a little more than twenty-four hours since he and Chloe had parted ways at the café. If he didn't know better, he'd think he was missing her.

An owl hooted in the distance as he approached the barn fence. The air was cool, but his denim jacket kept him warm enough not to notice. After checking a recent repair in the fence, he leaned against a post and admired the beautiful painted sky as the sun set low in the west.

He imagined his great-great-great-grandfather doing the same when he'd settled on this land back in the late 1800s. Generations of Holden men and women had watched the sun rise and set on Elk Creek Ranch, year after year, including his own father. That was part of the legacy that Cade wanted to share with his future wife and children. And why it was so important for him to get it right.

Still, he wasn't the kind of man to walk away from someone who needed help. And despite her strong protests, he believed Chloe needed lots of help to resolve this mess with Gino. He'd almost confided the truth to Nick yesterday at the Wildcat Tavern. Nick worked as a detective on the Pine City police force and might be able to offer Chloe some advice.

But how could he convince her that she needed his help? His desire to see her again was more than just physical attraction. She obviously didn't realize the trouble she could be in for concealing a criminal. Protecting her brother was one thing; aiding and abetting was quite another.

His own brothers weren't much help when he'd talked to them about Chloe. Not that he'd divulged anything about the jewels or criminal activity over beers with them yesterday. They'd beat the tar out of him if they thought he'd gone back to his outlaw ways.

No, he'd just wanted their advice about handling the woman Grandma Hattie had brought into his life. To his surprise, not one of them was sympathetic to his plight. Hank asked why he was so scared of a high-spirited filly like Chloe, and Jack said he'd acted like a darn fool with her at the café. Nick had stayed mostly silent about the subject and just sat there laughing to himself while drinking his beer. Cade thought about calling Sam, his bounty hunter brother, who was down in Galveston with his fiancée but figured he wouldn't be much help either.

That meant he had to figure this out on his own.

He took off his cowboy hat and raked one hand through his hair. Standing here ruminating wasn't getting him anywhere. He placed his hat back on, then turned and strode toward his pickup truck. Maybe driving around on some country roads would clear his head.

Twenty minutes later, he found himself in Pine City. Cade felt like a stalker cruising around Chloe's neighborhood, but he knew he had two choices. He could turn around and go home, or he could go after Chloe. Not that he wanted her in his life. She'd never be vanilla. But she did need his help. Especially since she was obviously still in denial about Gino.

He pulled up to a stop sign, letting the pickup truck idle as he contemplated which way to turn. Left would take him home. Right would take him to Chloe. He reminded himself that she didn't want to see him again. That the last time he'd shown up at Chloe's door, he'd been threatened with a knife, then bashed on the head. Left would be safer. Smarter. Duller.

He turned right.

Where was a cowboy when you really needed one? Or a horse that wouldn't get a flat tire? Chloe knelt by her car on the lone highway, tightening the last bolt on the spare tire with the tire iron. She still couldn't believe her bad luck. Wiping her damp brow with her jacket sleeve, she glanced down at her phone to see the time.

Damn. She was late.

She picked up the deflated tire and tossed it into her trunk, along with the tire iron. Then she slammed it shut and hopped into the driver's seat.

"Please be there, Gino," she implored under her breath. "Please wait for me."

Her entreaties grew more fervent with each mile. Traffic was light this evening, devoid of both cars and cows. That gave Chloe plenty of room to maneuver on the long stretch of highway.

A wave of apprehension swept through her. What if Gino didn't wait for her? What if she was too late? She pushed down on the gas pedal, watching the speedometer creep up. Seventy-six. Seventy-seven. Seventy-eight...

Speeding was a first for law-abiding Chloe, but tonight she felt compelled to break the law. She pushed it to eighty miles per hour, relieved her destination lay just up ahead. Then she glanced in her rearview mirror and her heart sank.

"This can't be happening," she groaned as she applied the brakes before easing the car onto the gravel shoulder.

The pulsating red lights of the police cruiser matched the beat of her heart. She rolled down the window as the deputy cautiously approached her car.

"Good evening, ma'am," he said, blinding her by shining the heavy-duty flashlight into her car. "I clocked you going eighty miles per hour in a seventy-five-mile-per-hour zone."

"I'm so sorry, but I can explain." Chloe leaned toward him, desperate for him to let her go with a just a warning.

He lifted his flashlight and swept the beam across the interior of her car. Judging by the implacable expression on the officer's craggy face, he was the suspicious type. She swallowed a sigh of exasperation. She didn't have time for delays. Gino would be long gone by the time she reached the Dairy Wizard. What if he didn't try to contact her again? What if he did something stupid?

"May I see your driver's license and registration, please?"

Chloe fumbled in her bag for her driver's license. "Again, I apologize, but I have a family emergency."

He perked up. "A medical emergency?"

"Not... yet," she said, seriously contemplating doing her little brother physical harm. She handed the deputy her license and the registration slip.

"Chloe Galetti," the deputy read, his eyes widening. "Are you any relation to Virgil Galetti? Or Marco Galetti? Or Ducky Galetti?"

She swallowed a groan. "Um... yes, as a matter of fact, I am."

He moved back from her car a pace, his expression suddenly wary. "Please step out of the vehicle, Ms. Galetti."

With a sinking sensation, Chloe did as he instructed. She'd heard her family tell stories before about the way law enforcement reacted to the Galetti name, but she'd never really believed them.

Until now.

Standing on the gravel shoulder at the rear of her car, she watched as the deputy did a quick search of the front and back seats. She briefly wondered if he needed a search warrant, but she didn't have time to question him about it.

She gritted her teeth when he made her open the trunk, his hand hovering near the butt of the pistol in his duty belt. Just the fact that her last name was Galetti made him expect trouble. Guilt by association.

After an interminable amount of time, the deputy finally let her go, forgetting, in his excitement of almost nabbing a Galetti, to give her a citation for speeding.

It was fifteen minutes past ten o'clock by the time Chloe reached the old, abandoned Dairy Wizard. Once a popular hangout for teenagers more than a decade ago, the Dairy Wizard now sat isolated and neglected at the end of a dead-end street. One of the streetlights was out, making the large, empty parking lot even spookier than it already was.

She got out of her car and peered around the murky shadows. There was no sign of Gino. There was no sign of anyone. A chill ran down her spine, even though she wore a warm jacket. She rubbed her hands up and down her arms. She didn't want to stay here alone, but she couldn't leave either. Not if there was at least the possibility Gino might still show up.

As her eyes adjusted to the darkness, she moved away from her car and closer to the Dairy Wizard. She skirted an upended aluminum trash can, almost jumping out of her shoes when a calico cat shot out of the can with a startled screech. She watched it run off into the thick hedge of rhododendron bushes that bordered the parking lot. It screeched again, louder this time, making the hairs prickle on the back of Chloe's neck.

She suddenly became aware of her own vulnerability. She was alone. At night. In a deserted parking lot. All five senses now on high alert, she continued toward the Dairy Wizard. She'd almost reached the plate glass front door when she saw it. A small, pristine white note taped to the outside of the door. She'd just plucked it off when she saw a shadow move out of the corner of her eye.

Gino.

Only it wasn't Gino. The man who rounded the corner of the building was bigger. Broader. Bleeding.

It was Cade.

He should have turned left.

Cade pulled a handkerchief out of his back pocket and mopped up the streak of blood running down his forearm. "What the hell do you think you're doing?"

"Me?" She stared at him. "What are you doing here?"

"Isn't it obvious?"

"It's obvious you followed me." She set her jaw. "I think I should warn you that stalking is a crime."

"Stalking? You think I'm stalking you?"

"Call me crazy. I suppose it's just coincidence that you showed up here in the middle of nowhere?"

"Maybe I wanted an ice-cream cone."

"You're too late. The Dairy Wizard closed nine years ago." Her gaze flicked to the long bleeding scratch on his arm. "Besides, it looks like you're more in need of a bandage than an ice-cream cone. What happened?"

He wiped away the last of the blood with his handkerchief, then stuck it in his back pocket. "Some stray cat jumped into the bushes and dug her claws into me."

Chloe arched a brow. "Her? How can you be so sure it was a female?"

"Because she was acting irrationally. Just like somebody else I know. Do you have any idea how dangerous it is for you to be out here alone?"

"I'm not alone. You're here."

"Only because I was smart enough to follow you."

"See," she exclaimed, stabbing one finger toward his chest, "you admit it. You've been following me."

"Damn straight. Good thing, too, considering your destination. You didn't even let a flat tire deter you."

Her brown eyes widened. "Wait a minute. You were there when I had the flat tire? I could have used some help."

"You handled it just fine." He stuffed the handkerchief back in his pocket. "Look, I didn't plan on following you. I drove up to your house just as you were pulling out of your driveway. That's when I decided to tag along." He took a step closer to her. "By the way, I was impressed by how fast you changed that flat tire."

"All the Galettis learn how to change a tire at a young age, just in case we need to make a quick getaway." She planted her hands on her hips. "But you still could have offered to help me."

"You're the one who said you don't like a man telling you what to do. I wasn't about to barge in and take over, especially since you happened to be holding a tire iron at the time." Little did she know that it had taken all his willpower to stay in his pickup truck and just watch her. But if he'd revealed himself, she never would have led him here. Cade still hadn't figured out the reason they were standing at a deserted Dairy Wizard on the outskirts of Pine City, but he knew something was up.

"And I suppose," she continued, "that you got a good chuckle when I was stopped for speeding, too."

His jaw tightened. "Believe me, I wasn't laughing. You were driving like a maniac. I thought only nuns drove that fast."

She blinked. "Excuse me?"

"Forget it. I'm just glad that deputy slowed you down."

"He slowed me down all right. Thanks to Pine City's finest, I missed Gino."

He stilled. "Gino was here?"

She hesitated for a brief moment. "Yes. That's why he called me last night. He wanted me to meet him here at ten o'clock and give him the diamonds. He sounded strange."

"Stranger than usual?"

"Yes, this was different. Gino has always been high-strung, but last night he sounded almost frantic."

"I'd be a little frantic, too, if I'd lost one hundred thousand dollars' worth of stolen diamonds. I'd certainly stick around long enough to see if my sister showed up with them. At the very least, I'd leave a note."

She looked up at him, her expression so sweet and innocent. "A note?"

"That's right," he said, moving another step closer to her. "Just like the one you've got hidden in your right hand."

She tucked her right arm behind her back. "I have no idea what you're talking about."

"Give it up, Galetti. You're a lousy liar. Besides, I've been watching you ever since I hunched down behind that hedge. I'm assuming that note is from Gino."

"How should I know?" She took two steps back from him. "I haven't even had time to read it yet."

"Then let's read it together. There's just enough light here." He motioned to the light pole above them.

Her brows furrowed. "Why?"

"Why what?"

"Why do you care what's in the note? Why did you follow me here?" She advanced on him until they stood toe-to-toe. "Why don't you just forget you ever met me?"

"I don't want to forget you," he said huskily, unable to stop from admitting it to her, much less himself. They'd only just met, but he couldn't stop thinking about her. Which was madness because the longer he was mixed up in this mess, the more he looked like an accomplice to a crime. And given his criminal record, he'd find himself right back in jail before it all got sorted out.

If it got sorted out.

But these past few days and nights, Chloe Galetti had filled his mind. Now she filled his senses. He could smell the subtle fragrance of her perfume. See the amber flecks in her brown eyes. Hear the beat of his own heart in his ears as he raised one hand and cupped her cheek, his fingers gently stroking over her soft, warm skin.

Right now, more than anything, he wanted to kiss her. But this was hardly the time or the place. Not when she was keeping secrets from him. Not when she still didn't trust him. He dropped his hand from her face. "Show me the note, Chloe."

She moistened her lips with her tongue, her gaze never leaving his. "On one condition. No matter what it says, I call the shots. Agreed?"

He opened his mouth to argue with her when a loud gunshot rang out. It shattered their reflections in the large plate glass window. Cade tackled Chloe, rolling so he took the brunt of the impact when they both hit the crumbling asphalt.

Another shot sounded, this bullet blasting through the big red plastic *D* on the Dairy Wizard sign just above their heads.

Cade held Chloe close to his chest. "Looks like someone else is calling the shots now."

Chloe stared at Cade, her cheeks drained of color. "Someone is trying to kill us."

"Lucky for us he's a lousy shot." He rolled away from her to upend the old picnic bench in front of them, using it as a barricade.

"He?" Chloe echoed, half sitting up. "You think it's Gino, don't you? You actually believe my brother is shooting at us!"

Cade pulled Chloe back down. "I'm not thinking anything right now, except how to get the hell out of here."

He kept his arm firmly around her waist to stop her from moving. He could feel the tension in her muscles, see the fast beat of the pulse in her throat.

"Listen," she whispered at last.

"I don't hear anything."

"Exactly. We might be safe now. Maybe whoever was shooting at us left."

"Or maybe he's just biding his time until he can get a clear shot."

"We can make a run for my car," she whispered.

"First, we need to douse the light." He looked up

at the light pole that illuminated the stretch of pavement between the Dairy Wizard and Chloe's car. "Otherwise, we'll be easy targets."

Chloe picked up a thick chunk of asphalt. "I'll give it a try."

"Let me," he said, taking it out of her hand.

She shrugged. "Okay, cowboy, here's your chance to impress me. Let's see if you can put out the light with one throw."

"And if I miss?"

"Then it's my turn."

He palmed the heavy chunk of asphalt in his hand. Taking a deep breath, he levered himself up and hurled it toward the light.

He missed.

"Forget it. This isn't going to work," Cade grumbled. "For one thing, I can't make an accurate throw from this position. For another, that lightbulb must be at least thirty feet high."

"Quit griping and give me some room," she whispered, picking up piece of asphalt and turning it over in her palm. She got to her feet, still hunched low behind the picnic table. Then her arm whipped up and around like a windmill, and she pitched the asphalt up toward the light.

A loud pop sounded right before the light went out.

"I don't believe it," he breathed as she dropped back down beside him. "What a lucky shot."

"No luck about it, cowboy. In high school, I was the starting pitcher on the girls' fast-pitch softball team. We qualified for the state tournament."

"Now you tell me."

"You didn't give me a chance before. You just went into your damsel-saving routine."

"That's what cowboys do." He grabbed her hand. "Now, do you want me to toss you over my shoulder before we make a run for it?"

"Keep dreaming and try to keep up with me," she said as they both took off.

They raced the short distance from the picnic table to the red coupe, Cade keeping his body between Chloe and the direction the shots had come from. She opened the front driver's door and dove headfirst inside the car, lying flat across the seat. Cade followed her into the car, barely managing to close the car door before landing on top of her.

"I can't breathe," she gurgled, her face pressed down against the seat cushion.

Cade levered himself up on his elbows, giving her enough room to turn onto her back. He lifted his head far enough to peer out the front windshield, searching the dark shadows for some sign of the shooter.

"Get down!" she whispered urgently, grabbing his shoulders and pulling him toward her.

He sank onto her soft, voluptuous body and his breathing hitched. They fit perfectly together. And at this moment, he couldn't think of anywhere he'd rather be. Chloe Galetti was brave and smart and sexy as hell. The adrenaline fueling his blood turned into something different. Something hot and molten and out of control. His heart raced and his body reacted with a will of its own.

She stared up into his face. "Kiss me."

"What?" he breathed, hardly able to believe his ears.

"Kiss me." She cradled his face in her hands. "I hate feeling scared. I want to feel... something else. Kiss me, Cade. Like you never want to stop."

With a low rumble of satisfaction, he did just as she asked. He kissed her, long and hard with no intention of stopping. He devoured her with his mouth, living for this moment alone. She kissed him back, matching his intense ferocity and serenading him with low moans of feminine desire.

At last, common sense battled its way through his dizzied senses. He lifted his head and took a deep, shuddering breath. "This is stupid. We're wasting time. We've got to get out of here."

She closed her eyes. "You're right. Get off me."

Easier said than done. But Cade finally managed to maneuver himself into a sitting position. "I'll drive. Give me the keys."

"No, I'll drive," Chloe countered, wedging herself behind him, then lunging into the driver's seat. "I'm shorter than you, it will be easier for me to hunch down behind the steering wheel."

She turned the key in the ignition before he had time to argue. Then she shifted the car into Drive and pushed the pedal to the floor. Cade jerked back as the car shot out of the parking lot.

"Is he following us?" Chloe asked, her eyes on the road.

He peered out the back window. "I don't see anyone, but keep driving."

"Where to?"

"My ranch."

Chloe shook her head. "All the shooter has to do is break into your pickup truck and look at your registration to get your address. And I don't think my place is safe, either."

"Then how about the police station? We can't play hide-and-seek with Gino anymore, Chloe. Somebody just tried to kill us."

Her hands tightened on the steering wheel, but to Cade's surprise, she didn't argue with him. He waited while she struggled to come to a decision.

"Maybe you're right," she said at last. "Maybe it's time to involve the police."

Chloe pulled into a deserted grocery store parking lot and turned off the ignition. Then she reached inside her purse for her cell phone. Her fingers shook as she dialed the number. Her whole body still trembled from the ordeal at the Dairy Wizard. Or from the aftereffects of Cade's kiss. She couldn't be certain which had shaken her more. She'd never been kissed like that. Ever.

Even worse, his kiss had done strange things to her. It made her feel giddy, confused, and out of control. Sensations she definitely wasn't used to feeling.

"Who are you calling?" he asked, watching her from the passenger seat.

"The police." Her hand tightened on the cell phone with the first ring.

He rubbed one hand over his jaw. "I guess I shouldn't be surprised you have the number memorized."

She flicked him a glance. "I guess not."

After the fourth ring, someone finally picked up on the other end. "Pine City Police Department.

How may I direct your call?"

She licked her lips. "I'd like to report a missing person."

"Your name, please?"

"Chloe Galetti. My brother, Gino Galetti, is the one who is missing." She heard Cade sputter beside her, but she ignored him. "I think he may be in danger."

"And is he a juvenile?"

"No, he's twenty-two years old."

"How long has he been missing, ma'am?"

"Almost forty-eight hours." She answered a few more routine questions, then ended the phone call.

"Well?" he asked.

She stuffed the cell phone back in her purse. "They want me to come down and file a missing person report."

"That's your idea of involving the police? Filing a missing person report? What about the fact that someone just took potshots at us? You also forgot to mention those hot diamonds hidden under your staircase. And the lousy remodeling job some creep did on your house."

Her eyes widened. "What about the note?"

"What note?"

She dug into her pocket. "The one on the Dairy Wizard door. I forgot all about it." Hardly surprising, considering the circumstances. First, she'd been distracted by the shooting, then Cade's kiss. She pulled out the crumpled paper and smoothed it out on the steering wheel.

He leaned over for a closer look. "What does it say?"

As she looked at the block letters, a chill ran down her spine. Then she read the words aloud, her voice sounding much calmer than she felt. "Saturday. Same time, same place. Bring the stash or you'll never see Gino again."

"It's a ransom note?" He shook his head. "That doesn't make any sense. Gino is the one who stole the diamonds in the first place."

"You were right before," she breathed. "Someone else is involved." Then she closed her eyes. "I should have known Gino could never pull off something this big by himself."

"And now it looks like his accomplice is holding Gino hostage."

She nodded, then opened her eyes. "To force me to turn over the diamonds. There's only one problem."

He arched a brow. "Only one?"

"All right," she conceded, leaning back against the headrest. "Several problems. Someone shot at us. My house isn't safe anymore. Your place isn't safe, either.

Gino is in danger. And..." Her voice trailed off as her throat grew tight.

"And?" he prompted.

She swallowed hard. "And I don't have the diamonds anymore."

Cade stared at her, his gut tightening with dread. "Please tell me you turned them over to the police."

"Not exactly."

"You didn't fence them, did you?"

"Of course not," she snapped, straightening in the seat. "Even I know you can't hock a fortune in diamonds in less than forty-eight hours."

"Then what did you do with them?"

"I mailed them."

He blinked. "You what?"

"I mailed them back to the jewelry store. I thought maybe if all the diamonds were returned, the police might drop the investigation and Gino would be cleared."

He dropped his head back against the seat with a groan of despair. Just when he thought matters couldn't get any worse, they always did. "I don't believe it. You mailed them. Didn't you consider the fact that they'll check both the diamonds and the bag for fingerprints? And they'll find Gino's. And yours." He lifted his head. "And mine."

She turned to face him. "Cade, you're talking to a Galetti. We learned to wipe our fingerprints off our baby bottles. The diamonds are clean and they're in a brand-new bag. I wore gloves and wiped down each diamond. Then I wrapped the bag in an old grocery sack, printed the address in block lettering on the padded envelope and dropped it in a mailbox five miles from my house."

He didn't say anything, obviously still looking for a flaw in her plan. At last, he said, "All right. It might work."

She shook her head. "No, it won't. We have to get those diamonds back."

"We have to go to the police," he countered. "I really mean it this time, Chloe. We're talking about kidnapping here. Not to mention assault with a deadly weapon."

"We're talking about the Galettis," she reminded him. "The police aren't going to bend over backward to help a Galetti. In fact, they'll probably try to implicate Gino in the shooting. And how can we possibly explain the ransom note without mentioning the diamonds?" She shook her head. "We have to handle this one on our own."

"We?"

She sucked in her breath. But why should she be surprised? What man in his right mind would volunteer to become entangled in this complicated, not to mention dangerous, mess? Cade had already stuck with her longer than she'd expected. It had been so nice. Especially after spending so many years trying to solve the Galetti family problems on her own.

Time for a reality check.

"Not we," she amended as she switched on the car ignition. "This is my problem, not yours. Is there some place safe I can drop you until this all blows over? Can you stay with your grandmother or one of your brothers?"

"Blows over?" He stared at her in disbelief. "Chloe, I think you're missing the seriousness of the situation. This isn't going to just blow over. Try blow up."

"All right, blow up. I know you don't want to be caught in the explosion. And you certainly don't want to be around to pick up the pieces."

"How do you know what I want?" His voice sounded low and husky, causing prickles of awareness to spread over her body.

"So, tell me," she said.

"I don't know." He raked one hand through his hair. "I've been confused ever since the night we met. All I know right now is that I don't want either one of us to get shot at again. And I don't want you trying to save Gino by yourself."

"I doubt you want to commit a federal offense by breaking into a mailbox, either."

"Damn straight. There's got to be another way." He peered out the window, as if suddenly aware the car was moving. "Where are we going?"

"Someplace safe. Then we can decide exactly what to do."

"A hotel?"

"Not exactly."

"Then where, exactly?"

"The Galetti safe house." She glanced over at him in time to see his jaw drop. "The Galettis have used it for years as a place to hide out when things get a little too hot."

"A safe house," he muttered under his breath. "Unbelievable."

"Well, it's not exactly a house."

"Then what is it?"

Chloe merged onto Interstate 70, the lights of the city now in her rearview mirror. "Years ago, my great-uncle, Paul Galetti, bought a farm near Grubville to raise Angora sheep. He was actually legit."

"Imagine that."

She ignored the sarcasm. "Anyway, Uncle Paul's place provided a safe haven for some of the more...

nefarious Galettis. A tornado wiped out most of it in 1964 and Uncle Paul gave up the Angoras and moved back to the city. But he never sold the land, so the Galettis still use it as a hideout."

"Don't tell me we're going to stay in a barn."

"Of course not. The hideout is underground." She flashed him a wry smile. "I hope you're not claustrophobic."

8

Cade couldn't believe his eyes. Chloe hadn't exaggerated. The Galetti hideout really was underground. It was an old root cellar that had been used to store food before refrigeration had come along. From the outside it looked just like the storm cellar in *The Wizard of Oz*, where everyone but Dorothy had hidden during the tornado.

Chloe had led him to an old, faded pine door set in a slab of cement. He hadn't even noticed it among the overgrown brush and dozens of cedar trees until he almost tripped over it. She pulled the door open, then they descended a steep flight of concrete steps into the surprisingly spacious room below. Cade could even stand at his full height without having to crouch.

"This is amazing," he said, looking around the cozy interior. A sofa sat snugly against one wall, covered with a hand-crocheted blue afghan. The floor was hard-packed dirt, covered almost wall-to-wall with a bright paisley area rug. The plaster walls had a fresh coat of whitewash and rows of canned goods and pantry items lined the shelves near the entrance.

"This is the only place on the farm that survived the tornado. The Galettis have fixed it up over the years to make it more habitable." She pointed toward a folding accordion door. "My cousin Lenny even put in a bathroom that operates on an antigravity system. He's a plumber."

"So, he's legit, too?"

"Most of the time." Chloe slipped out of her shoes, then curled up on one end of the sofa. She hid a huge yawn behind her hand.

"Tired?" Cade asked, joining her on the sofa. "The adrenaline must finally be wearing off." He leaned forward, resting his elbows on his knees. "We still have some decisions to make."

"I know." Her voice sounded tired and flat. "I guess I was hoping we might find Gino here. That the ransom note was some kind of hoax. That somehow everything would work itself out and I could go back to my regularly scheduled life." She looked up at him. "But that's not going to happen, is it?"

"No, Chloe," he said gently. "That's not going to happen."

She sighed. "I don't want to think about it anymore tonight. My head is already spinning. Let's talk about something else." Her mouth quirked up in a half smile. "Let's talk about you."

"Me?" he said in surprise.

"Time to spill your deep, dark secrets, cowboy. It's only fair since you know so much about the Galetti family."

"I already told you about my outlaw past, and you've met my grandmother and my brother Jack. What else do you want to know?"

She drew up her knees and wrapped her arms around them. "Tell me about your list."

"My list?"

"Gino told me you have a list of requirements for the perfect wife." She chuckled. "Is that true?"

"I wouldn't exactly call them requirements," he hedged. "Compatibility is important in a relationship. When I marry, I want it to be forever."

Her smiled softened. "Oh, that's really nice. And not very common these days."

"That's why I have a list. I figured if I wrote down

some of the attributes that I find attractive in a woman, that might help me increase my odds of getting it right."

He didn't mention the attributes he currently found attractive—none of which had made his list. Deep-brown eyes. A quick wit and fiery independent streak. A mouth that made him burn for her. And he was more than ready to leap back into the fire.

"Such as?" she asked thoughtfully.

Cade cleared his throat and forced himself to look away from her mouth. "Such as... loyalty, like we mentioned before. Family loyalty is very important to me."

She nodded. "I can't argue with that one. What else?"

He thought about how the rest of his list would sound to Chloe, and now it suddenly seemed dumb to him. That's when he decided to turn the tables on her. "What do you think is on it?"

"Well, just in the short time we've known each other, I'm pretty sure I can guess." She gave him a playful smile. "Great legs. A killer body. Adept in the kitchen *and* the bedroom. Oh, and a talent for vacuuming."

He shifted uncomfortably on the sofa. Her wild guesses were a little too close for comfort. "Very funny. But for your information, I'm a pretty good cook and I can wrangle a vacuum better than anyone."

"You're full of it," she said, laughing.

"You don't believe me?" He looked around the root cellar. "Do you have a vacuum cleaner down here? Because I'd be happy to give you a one-man show."

"That does sound fun, but there's no vacuum." She tilted her head to one side, studying him. "You're serious, aren't you?"

"Completely serious." He leaned back on the sofa and put his feet up on the ottoman. "I learned to vacuum when I was about twelve years old and looking for trouble wherever I could find it. Grandma Hattie put me to work doing household tasks just to keep me busy. She taught me how to vacuum, cook, bake, and do laundry. At the time, I hated every minute of it." Then he chuckled. "But not as much as I hated Grandpa Henry's form of punishment."

"Did it involve taking you behind the woodshed?"

He shook his head. "Nope, Grandpa Henry was much more creative than that. He'd make me toss a fifty-pound feed sack over the barn fence. Then I'd have to climb over the fence and pick up that same feed sack and toss it back over to the other side."

"That is creative," she mused.

"Oh, I'm not done," he said with a smile. "I had to throw that feed sack back and forth fifty times in a row. I could take as many breaks as I wanted, but there was a price."

She leaned forward, her gaze fixed on him. "What kind of price?"

"Grandpa Henry would teach me life lessons while I hurled that heavy feed sack around. He'd talk about a wide variety of subjects, like the right way to treat a lady and how to not break my hand in a fist fight. Things like that." Cade cleared his throat. "I still remember the day he went into embarrassing detail about the birds and the bees. That day was the fastest I ever threw that feed sack over the fence. I finished up in record time."

She laughed, but something about his story made her heart melt. For the first time since she'd met Cade Holden, she realized she could be in danger of falling in love with him. He might be opinionated and obstinate—not to mention a little clueless about women—but he was also the man who had stuck with her through an assault with a deadly weapon. No, two assaults with deadly weapons. He hadn't turned her brother over to the police or abandoned her or even questioned why she'd go to such lengths for her crazy family.

"Now it's your turn," he said, turning to Chloe.

"My turn?"

"That's right. You know about my secret vacuuming powers. That's blackmail material. If I don't have equal ammunition, I'll be completely at your mercy."

She swallowed at the image his words provoked. The cave suddenly seemed much smaller than before. And warmer. The night stretched before them, long and dark and intimate. She sucked in a deep breath, suddenly very aware it was just the two of them here.

"Quit stalling," he prodded, his grin telling her he had no idea what she was thinking.

Good. For once, she was glad he was clueless. Because she needed to think long and hard about these new feelings welling up inside of her. "You already know about the Galetti secret hideout," she began. "You're the first outsider to be admitted, by the way. You should be honored."

He slowly shook his head. "I'm not talking about a Galetti family secret. I want a secret about you. Something you've never told anyone."

Her entire life had been full of secrets. When your father was a jewel thief and your mother was an aspiring con artist, you learned to keep your mouth shut. But Cade already knew about the notorious

Galetti family. He wanted something more. Something just about her.

"There is one thing I've never told anyone," she said softly.

"Until now," he added with a mischievous grin.

"Until now," she agreed, finding his smile contagious. Then she took a deep breath, preparing herself to reveal something that she had buried deep in her heart six years ago. "When I was twenty-one, I fell madly in love."

A muscle ticked in his jaw. "I see."

"And we eloped."

Cade blinked. "Oh."

She laughed aloud at his expression. "Are you surprised someone would want to marry me?"

"Of course not."

His brisk tone surprised her. "Do you want to hear the rest of my secret or not?"

"Sure," he said. "Just spare me the honeymoon details."

"There wasn't a honeymoon. Because there wasn't a wedding. I'd neglected to tell my true love the true facts about the Galetti family. But I didn't want any secrets in our marriage, so I spilled everything on the day of the wedding."

"How did he handle it?"

"Fine. Until we got in front of the officiant. Then

he got a case of cold feet—or maybe a vision of his feet in cement. I tried to explain to him that just because we have Italian ancestry doesn't mean we're a part of the Mafia. But he was running out of the chapel by that time, so I don't think he heard me."

Cade met her gaze. "Sounds like tonight wasn't the first time you dodged a bullet. You almost married a fool and a coward."

She shook her head. "No, it was my fault for not telling him sooner. Plus, he'd seen *The Godfather* one too many times and had an overactive imagination."

"Well, I still say it's his loss."

She looked up at him, surprised by his vehemence. "Thank you, Cade. I think that's the nicest thing you've ever said to me."

He looked surprised. "I say nice things to you all the time."

Her mouth dropped open. "Like what?"

"Like… you've got a great house."

"You're hopeless," she said, laughing. But at least she wasn't angry with him like she'd been earlier in the evening. Just the opposite, in fact. She was falling hard and fast for the man.

And that was one secret Chloe intended to keep to herself.

Cade held his breath as Chloe's eyelids drooped and a soft sigh escaped her lips. She was asleep. Finally. In the last few hours, it had taken all his willpower not to take her in his arms. Not to look at her as if she were a sinful dessert and he was a starving man. Now he could watch her to his heart's content as she lay curled up on the sofa. He'd been testing himself—proving to himself that he could resist Chloe Galetti.

He'd passed, but it didn't give him any satisfaction.

Moving with quiet deliberation, he picked up the blue afghan off the back of the sofa and gently laid it on top of her. For the first time in his life, he envied a blanket. He wanted to be the one on top of her. Keeping her warm—among other things.

With a silent sigh of frustration, he dragged his fingers through his hair. He'd never wanted a woman this badly. Especially a woman like her. He turned away from her and began to pace back and forth across the narrow root cellar.

What was it about Chloe that drew him?

He knew it was more than desire. He'd experienced physical attraction before, although never quite this intense. All it took was one look from her, just a touch, to set his senses whirling. Still, any man could see she was a stunning woman. Cade now realized that there was more to Chloe than great curves and a dynamite pair of legs. She had a good heart. A stalwart spirit. And a talent for making things beautiful.

His pacing slowed as he pondered the fact that none of those qualities were on his list. How could he possibly have valued a pair of great legs above a sense of humor? A silly list above love?

He froze. *Love?*

Of course not! Impossible. Ridiculous. Still, his heart pounded in his chest as he began pacing once again. He could never love someone like Chloe. She might be wonderful, but their lives were so different. She was a Galetti. And he was old enough to know you didn't just marry the woman, you married the family. That was one of the life lessons Grandpa Henry had taught him. But the thought of Gino as his brother-in-law was almost unbearable.

Almost.

Cade sank down in a beige recliner, the velour fabric worn almost threadbare on the seat and arms. He buried his face in his hands and took a deep breath. It was late and he was exhausted. This was probably not the best time to contemplate his future.

Especially with Chloe so close to him.

He lifted his head and looked his fill, knowing he might never see her this way again. He memorized the way her long, dark lashes fanned out on her creamy cheeks. The way her slender fingers curled around the throw pillow. He listened to her soft, somnolent breathing until the rhythm matched the beat of his heart.

Now, at this moment, he could let his imagination run wild. Pretend Chloe was his. For now. For always. Dream about watching her fall asleep every night, then awaken in his arms every morning. Tomorrow was soon enough for reality. Tomorrow Chloe would be lost to him forever.

Tomorrow he planned to report her brother to the police as the diamond thief.

Cade woke up slowly, his muscles stiff and his right arm numb. He blinked twice, trying to orient himself to his surroundings. Then he remembered. He was in a root cellar with Chloe Galetti. He sat up in the recliner as he inhaled the aroma of brewing coffee. An LED light on the ceiling illuminated the makeshift kitchen in the corner of the room, but Chloe was nowhere in sight.

He stood up, every muscle in his body protesting the fact that he'd used the recliner as a bed. Then he stretched his arms over his head and yawned.

The cellar door creaked open above him. "Chloe?"

"Morning, sleepyhead," she called as she climbed down the cellar steps, a grocery sack in each arm.

He hurried to take them from her. "Where have you been?"

"I couldn't stomach the thought of powdered eggs and canned sausages for breakfast, so I made a quick trip to Sully's Convenience Mart. It's only about a five-minute drive."

"I thought we were in hiding."

She shrugged. "I took a chance that Sully wasn't the one shooting at us yesterday. I like to live on the edge."

"Tell me about it," he muttered, setting the grocery sacks on the table.

"Are you always this cheerful in the morning?"

"I didn't sleep too well."

"You should have shared the sofa with me." She began unloading the groceries. "There was plenty of room."

He might not have slept well in the rocking chair, but the thought of cuddling up next to Chloe wasn't exactly sleep-inducing, either.

He cleared his throat. "What's for breakfast?"

"Take your pick." She motioned to the assorted boxes and packages on the table. "I stocked up on cherry Pop-Tarts, chocolate donuts, and diet soda."

He grimaced. "You call that breakfast?"

"Every day," she quipped, popping the tab on her soda can.

He peeked into a grocery sack. But the only thing he found inside was the morning newspaper. Grabbing a chocolate glazed donut from the box, he sat down at the table with the newspaper in front of him. Cade had just taken his first bite when he saw the headline. He choked, his airway constricted by donut and disbelief.

"Here," Chloe said, quickly pushing her soda toward him. "Drink this."

He washed down the donut, then took a deep breath as he slowly wiped his mouth with the back of his hand.

"Hey, are you okay?" she asked, her eyes clouded with concern.

"No." He turned the newspaper toward her. "I'm not okay. In fact, my life just took a decided turn for the worse."

Chloe picked up the paper and read the front-page headline aloud. "*Suspect Sought In Jewel Heist.*" The paper dropped onto the table as the concern in her eyes turned to panic. "Gino. They're after Gino!"

"Wrong." Cade pushed the paper toward her. "They're after me."

She blinked at him. "You?"

He pointed at the front page. "Read the first paragraph."

She picked up the newspaper again, her forehead furrowed. Then she began reading aloud. *"Local rancher Cade J. Holden is being sought for questioning in the recent burglary of Akana Jewelers. Mr. Holden was last seen on Sunday, January 14th. That evening, his abandoned vehicle was found hidden near the parking lot of the closed Dairy Wizard on Farmington Road. Police sources report that a small ruby was discovered in the glove compartment of Holden's vehicle. The ruby has since been identified as one of the items stolen from the jewelry store."*

She slowly lowered the paper. "A ruby? There weren't any rubies in the bag of diamonds we found. And rubies weren't mentioned in the last newspaper article."

His jaw clenched. "It's possible other jewels were stolen from Akana's in that burglary and hidden separately from the diamonds. Sounds like the police held back that information to either throw off the thief or to weed out false confessions."

"What makes you think that?"

"I have a lot of experience with cops, remember?"

"And I've done everything I can to avoid them." Chloe sank down onto the chair across from him. "The real thief must have planted the ruby in your pickup truck the night he shot at us."

"The real thief?"

She looked up at him, then slowly shook her head. "No. It's not Gino."

"How can you be so sure?"

She sighed. "I hate to admit it, but my brother simply isn't that smart."

"He's not exactly innocent, either. Gino is the one who arranged the meeting at the Dairy Wizard last night. He not only knows about the diamonds but seems willing to do almost anything to get them back."

She rubbed her fingers over her temple. "I agree that he looks guilty. Our father used to tell us bedtime stories about his most exciting burglary jobs and how they ended happily—and richly— ever after. Gino soaked up every word."

Bedtime stories? Cade couldn't believe it. No wonder Gino had problems. Growing up among the Galettis must have been hard enough, but to glamorize a life of crime and make it sound like a fairy tale bordered on child abuse. And Chloe had suffered, too. She'd missed most of her childhood, forced to grow up too soon when her mother went off to jail. And she was still trying to pick up the pieces.

It hit him then, what a truly amazing woman she was. With all her family's problems, she'd still managed to put herself through college and start her own business. The temptation to join the Galettis' more lucrative, if illegal, ventures must have been almost overwhelming. Yet she'd resisted the lure of easy money and excitement. Even after losing her mother to prison. Her father to a heart attack. And her cowardly fiancé to cold feet.

There was no doubt about it. Chloe Galetti was a truly incredible woman. She was also deluding herself if she believed Gino wasn't up to his kneecaps in this quagmire.

"But here's the thing, Cade," she continued. "The thief shot at us, and I know in my heart Gino would never do that."

"Unless he was shooting at me and not you."

"Think about it," she said, obviously seeing the skepticism on his face. "You know my brother. Do you really think Gino could pull off something this diabolical? Frame you for a crime you didn't commit? Hold himself hostage in a ruse to get the diamonds back? Shoot at his own sister?"

"He missed, remember?"

"Barely. Besides, Gino is terrified of guns. Which always put a damper on his gangster fantasies."

"If Gino isn't involved, then who is?"

She shook her head. "I don't know. But one thing I do know is that if Gino is implicated in any of this, it could ruin my mother's chance for parole."

"Why should that even be a factor?"

"Because the Galetti name will be in the newspapers. Again. And no doubt the reporters will dredge up all their past mishaps as well. What civic-minded parole board would put another Galetti back on the street?"

He couldn't argue with her logic because she was probably right. Today, politicians got elected for their tough-on-crime stance. Especially for habitual offenders like Chloe's mother. Eileen Galetti's chances for making parole would be slim to none once it was known that her son had followed in her footsteps.

"You can't keep making excuses for Gino," he said with quiet deliberation. "You can't keep trying to save him, or he'll never learn how to stand on his own two feet."

"He'll be standing in a chain gang if I don't do something!"

"You're the one who's in prison," Cade snapped, irritated with her misguided loyalty and his own feelings of helplessness. "Trapped by your brother and your mother and all those other Galettis who keep you from pursuing your own dreams. You can't be their conscience forever, Chloe. You have to start looking out for yourself."

"Maybe." She swallowed hard. "But if I let Gino go to prison, I'll be..."

He reached for her hand, his irritation fading when he saw the slight tremor of her lower lip. "You'll be what?"

"I'll be... alone."

He held on tight to her hand. "You're not alone."

She gave him a watery smile. "Thanks, cowboy. I take back all those things I said about you."

"What things?"

"That you're hardheaded, opinionated, bossy. They're still true," she added, "but I'm sorry I said them out loud. I should have at least included your good traits, too." She traced her thumb lightly over his knuckles. "You're handsome, honest, reliable, and smart. You're also incredibly calm considering the fact that the police have probably impounded your pickup truck."

"And now I'm a wanted man." Her touch made his breath catch. "Maybe I'm still in shock. Or maybe..." His voice trailed off as he stared into her eyes. They were so deliciously brown, like melted chocolate. Everything about her was delicious. His gaze fell to her lips, and he suddenly knew exactly what he wanted for breakfast.

"Maybe what?" she asked, her lips parting in surprise as he suddenly stood and pulled her to him.

"Maybe I can't think about anything except kissing you again." He bent his head and captured her mouth, savoring its sweetness. He moaned with the pleasure of a man who had finally satisfied his craving. After the long night of self-denial, he let himself fully indulge in Chloe Galetti.

She tasted warm and wonderful. He wrapped his arms around her, marveling again at how perfectly she fit against him. Her hands swept through his hair, her nails lightly raking the nape of his neck. The sensation brought his entire body to full alert. He deepened the kiss, one hand trailing over the smooth curve of her hip.

She moaned low in her throat and that sound alone almost sent him over the edge. Her fingers tugged at the front of his shirt and somewhere in the far reaches of his mind he realized she was undoing the buttons. Now it was his turn to moan when her hand slipped inside his shirt and brushed over the hair on his chest.

He couldn't stand it anymore. More to the point, he couldn't stand up anymore. He wanted Chloe on the sofa. Under him, on top of him, it didn't make any difference. As long as she was touching him. As long as they were together.

He edged them closer to the sofa, their lips still clinging together, their hands still discovering the most exquisite places. Only one more step and all those hot, erotic dreams he'd been having since meeting Chloe would finally come true.

Then he heard the cellar door slam open above them, followed by the voice that gave him nightmares.

"Get your hands off my sister!"

9

"I said get your hands off her!" Gino snapped as he limped down the stairs and moved slowly toward them.

"Gino!" Chloe stepped out of Cade's arms, hastily pulling her clothing back into place. "What happened? Are you hurt?"

She barely recognized her brother. His long hair hung loose and tangled around his face. He wore the same black denim jeans and sky-blue hoodie he'd been wearing the last time she'd seen him. And there were dark circles under his eyes.

"Gino, answer me? Are you okay?" Chloe reached out and grabbed her brother's bony shoulders, giving him a light shake. Then her gaze swept over his rail-thin body. No blood. No broken bones. No sign of any permanent damage that she could see.

"Ouch!" Gino yelped, wriggling out of her grasp. "I'm fine. Let me go." Then he frowned at her as he rubbed one hand over his right shoulder. "You scratched me. I hate those long fingernails."

"She can't scratch you through your hoodie," Cade told him. He stood where she'd left him, his shirt still unbuttoned and his chest rising up and down from their passionate encounter. "How did you know we were here? Did anyone follow you?"

"Chloe dug her nails into me really hard," Gino said, ignoring his questions. "She's done that since we were little."

"Well, you're not little anymore." Cade took a menacing step toward him. "Now why don't you..."

"Sit down here," Chloe quickly interjected, patting the sofa beside her, "and tell us everything that's happened to you." She wanted to defuse the situation, hoping Gino had already forgotten what he'd seen from the open cellar door. Her heart still beat a rapid tattoo in her chest and her mouth tingled from Cade's kiss.

Her brother always did have lousy timing.

Gino winced and moaned with every step, then slumped onto the sofa cushion with an air of exhaustion. "I can't believe I made it here alive."

Cade took his time buttoning up his shirt. "You

may not stay that way if you don't give us some answers."

"Me?" Gino stuck out his chin. "I'm the one who should be demanding answers. Such as—what exactly were you doing to my sister just now?"

Cade leveled his gaze on Chloe and the desire in his blue eyes made her stomach flip-flop. "I think that's obvious."

"I think it's disgusting." Gino turned to Chloe. "I told you to stay away from him. You never listen to me."

"I'm listening now," she said, leaning toward him. "So, it's time to start talking. Who stole the diamonds? Who knocked Cade out? Who broke into our house and turned it upside down? And what I'd really like to know is who decided to use Cade and me for target practice out by the Dairy Wizard?"

Gino rubbed his forehead with his fingers. "I have a horrendous headache. And you're yelling at me."

She took a deep breath and tried to calm down. It was all happening too fast. From the moment she'd met Cade Holden, her life and her emotions had started spinning out of control. If Gino hadn't appeared at exactly the wrong moment, she would have followed Cade anywhere. Specifically, onto the sofa. She looked at it with longing, her body still thrumming with unfulfilled desire.

Then she mentally shook herself. Her love life, or lack of one, should be the last thing on her mind right now. Her brother was here. He was safe. He needed her.

"I'm sorry I yelled at you," she said more calmly. "Would you like a soda or something to eat?"

Gino looked up at her, his puppy-brown eyes suddenly eager. "Yes, I'm starving. Do you have any Fig Newtons? I've been dying for a Fig Newton."

"No, we don't," she replied, half standing up, "but I can run down to the store..."

"Stop coddling him," Cade interjected, a muscle knotting his jaw. "He'll survive without Fig Newtons." Then he turned to her brother. "Gino, you need to get it together."

"Cade," she scolded, "he's hurt. Just look at him."

Gino stared up at his sister. "He's never liked me."

"That's not true," Cade countered, folding his arms across his chest. "And even if it was, I happen to like your sister. She's been worried sick about you." His brows snapped together. "So, stop thinking about yourself for a change and think about her."

"All I can think about is you and her together like that..." A fiery blush suffused Gino's cheeks. "She's never been that kind of girl until she met you."

Chloe's own cheeks warmed at his implication.

"Please stop worrying about me, Gino. Nothing happened."

"Like hell," Cade muttered beside her.

"Well, that's a relief," Gino looked skeptical. "If it's true." He rose to his feet and approached Cade. "Okay. You can go home now. I'll take care of my sister."

Chloe was getting a little tired of the macho protector act—from both men. She was almost ready to kick them out of the root cellar. "In case you two big, strong men haven't noticed, this little lady is perfectly capable of taking care of herself."

"She's right," Cade said evenly, his gaze fixed on Gino. "If you don't mind, I think I'll stick around here a little while longer."

Gino's nostrils flared. "And if I do mind?"

"Then I'll be happy to discuss it with you outside." Cade nodded toward the cellar stairs. "Your choice."

Gino slumped back down onto the sofa. "All right. I'll let you stay." Then he winced as he slowly lifted his leg and propped it on top of the coffee table. "Do you have any ice here, Chloe?"

"No." She bent down to examine his ankle, carefully pushing up the hem of his jeans and trying to ignore his agonized groans. Her brother might act immaturely, but Cade wasn't helping the situation.

She looked up at him and their eyes met. "*Be nice to him,*" she mouthed silently.

Then she turned her attention back to her brother. "Your ankle doesn't look bruised or swollen."

"But it really hurts," Gino said, his face contorting with pain. "Do you think it's broken?"

"No, it's not broken." Cade knelt by the sofa and studied his ankle. "It's probably just a high sprain. You'd be hurting a heck of a lot more if it was broken; take it from me. I broke my left ankle two years in a row."

Gino looked at Cade, curiosity gleaming in his eyes. "For real?"

"I'm afraid so. I did plenty of dumb things when I was your age."

"But how did you break it twice?" Gino asked him.

Chloe noticed that Cade's tone was gentler now and his breathing steady and even. He also seemed to realize that the best way to get information from Gino was to engage him in conversation instead of trying to force it out of him.

"I used to compete in bull-riding with the local rodeo circuit." Cade moved to a chair and stretched his long legs out in front of him. "It seemed like an easy way to make some extra money. Also, it was a good way to keep me out of trouble." His gaze flicked to Chloe, then back to Gino again. "There was this one bull named Crash and he was my nemesis."

Gino's eyes widened. "Did that bull buck you off him?"

"He sure did. I went flying through the air. Then he came after me when I hit the ground and stomped a hoof on my left ankle. I could hear the bone break."

Chloe grimaced, but Gino seemed fascinated.

"And you broke your ankle the next year too?" Gino asked.

Cade nodded. "Same ankle, but this time it was Crash's offspring, a young bull named Firecracker."

Chloe listened in fascination, although she wondered if Cade was embellishing the story for her brother's sake. "I'm surprised you can walk normally."

His mouth curved into a half smile as he looked at her. "I spent all my rodeo winnings on physical therapy, but my ankle is almost as good as new." He lifted his left leg in the air and made a circle with his foot. "See, no permanent damage done."

Gino nodded, obviously impressed. "Good thing I dropped that power saw on your right foot then, isn't it? Otherwise, you might need more physical therapy."

"That's one way to look at it," Cade said dryly. "Now tell us how you hurt your ankle."

"I twisted it trying to escape," Gino said.

"Escape?" Chloe's heart clenched. "From your kidnappers?"

Gino's straggly dark brows drew together as he turned to his sister. "Kidnappers? Where did you get a crazy idea like that?"

"From this ransom note we found." Cade pulled the sheet of paper out of his shirt pocket. "Are you telling us no one has been holding you against your will?"

"Of course not. That's crazy." Gino looked between the two of them. "I've been staying at the Whistling Duck Motel out by Route 82, and somehow I got locked in the bathroom. The only way I could escape was through the window. It must have been at least a six-foot drop to the ground."

Now Chloe was more confused than ever. She'd assumed her brother hadn't been able to contact her. Instead, it sounded like he'd been on vacation. "What have you been doing at the Whistling Duck? I've been worried sick about you."

"You're not going to like it," Gino warned her.

"Tell us anyway," Cade said, settling in for a long story. "We're getting used to bad news."

"I consider this good news." Gino cleared his throat, then rose awkwardly to his feet. "Nanette and I are back together. For keeps, this time."

Chloe's mouth dropped open. "Nanette Twigg? I heard she moved to Florida."

"She did," Gino confirmed, "until I convinced her to come back to Pine City." The corners of his mouth twitched. "I guess she just can't stay away from the man she loves."

Chloe shook her head, not certain where to begin. "Nanette is all wrong for you, Gino."

"Well, I happen to think Cade Holden is all wrong for you," he retorted.

"She's a convicted felon!"

"So is he."

"She was in prison for attempted murder."

"Nobody's perfect." He shrugged his shoulders. "Besides, Nanette's conviction was overturned on a technicality."

She threw her arms up in the air. "That doesn't mean she's not guilty! It just means somebody made a mistake along the way and she got lucky."

"Nanette deserves a little luck," he insisted. "She's had a rough life and her last husband made her miserable."

"Is that why she put rat poison in his oatmeal?" Chloe could see Cade's head moving back and forth as they spoke, like he was watching a tennis match. But she was too upset with Gino to care.

"He didn't eat it," Gino said in defense of his girlfriend. "Claimed the oatmeal was too lumpy. Nanette said he was the pickiest eater she'd ever met."

"Lucky for him," Cade quipped. "It's time to start letting your brain do your thinking, Gino, instead of your—"

"I think," Chloe said, cutting off Cade midsentence, "that we'd better start from the beginning. Gino, what really happened at Akana Jewelers?"

Gino smiled. "You never believed I could pull it off, did you, sis?"

The words made her heart plummet. This whole time she'd been trying to convince herself that Gino was innocent. "I was hoping you didn't do it, but now..." Her voice broke and she covered her mouth with her hand. She could sense Cade moving closer to her, but she shook her head and turned away from him.

Gino's eyes widened as he got off the sofa. "Please don't cry, Chloe. As much as I hate to admit it, I can't take the credit for the break-in at Akana's. Nanette did it all."

"She did?" Chloe breathed. Relief washed over her when she realized Gino hadn't followed in their father's footsteps. Not yet anyway.

"If Nanette stole the diamonds," Cade asked, "how did they end up under the staircase in your house?"

"She hid them there," Gino explained. "Only I didn't know it at the time. She showed up at our front door about a week ago and told me she still loved me and wanted a chance to win me back. She must have hidden the diamonds while I was upstairs changing for our date."

"Oh, Gino," Chloe said with a groan of frustration. "She was just using you. Can't you see that?"

"Let him tell it, Chloe," Cade said gently, now standing beside her. His hand found the back of her neck, and he gently massaged the tight muscles there. She realized then how tense she'd gotten since Gino had started his story. She was so afraid it wasn't going to have a happy ending.

"Nanette really does love me," Gino insisted. "In fact, it's my fault she stole the diamonds in the first place. See"—he took a deep breath—"it was my idea. My plan. We used to write letters to each other about it when she was in prison." He glanced at Cade. "Using a secret code, of course. I'm not stupid."

"Go on," Cade urged him.

"Well, I suppose I was showing off in a way," Gino said, "trying to impress her with all my knowledge about how to be a master jewel thief. I never really meant for us to go through with it. After all, she was serving fifteen-to-twenty years. I thought she'd forget all about it by the time she got out."

"Only Nanette got out sooner, and she didn't forget about it," Chloe said.

"Yep," Gino affirmed, misery etched on his face. "She actually went through with it."

Chloe's shock was fading, replaced by a growing anger. "Is she the one who hit Cade over the head?"

He nodded. "She came to the back door that night and asked if I was home alone. I told her you were upstairs and the jerk who fired me was in the living room. She came inside and almost lost it when she saw Cade looking under the staircase. The next thing I knew, she'd picked up the Chihuahua and bashed him in the head."

"I could kill her," Chloe muttered under her breath.

"I was upset, too," Gino replied. "She broke my Chihuahua's ear."

"She didn't do my head a lot of good either," Cade intoned. "But go on with your story."

Gino glanced nervously between his sister and Cade. "Well, I freaked out when I saw you lying there on the floor. I mean, you looked *very* dead. Then we heard Chloe at the top of the stairs, and I guess we both panicked and ran."

"But not before stealing my wallet," Cade added.

"It fell out while we were shoving you under the stairs," he explained. "Nanette said the cash and credit cards might come in handy. Especially if we had to go on the lam."

"Oh, Gino." Chloe closed her eyes in despair.

"I know," Gino said with a sheepish glance at his sister. "But you know I don't handle a crisis well. And Nanette was practically hysterical. That's when she told me about the diamonds and how it had been a big mistake to leave them at our house. We were at the Whistling Duck Motel by then, and well, one thing led to another..."

"I think we can skip this part," Cade said dryly.

"Anyway, I fell asleep," Gino continued. "Later, I found out that Nanette went back to the house to get the diamonds. Only she couldn't find them."

"Did she have to tear the house to pieces looking for them?" Chloe asked. "The place is a disaster area."

Gino shrugged. "I guess she panicked again. I mean, she was acting pretty paranoid by that point. She was even worried about the letters she'd sent me from prison. I told her I'd saved them all."

"Could they implicate her in the robbery?" Cade asked him.

"Well, yeah, especially before we started writing in code. I mean, she asked a lot of questions initially. And she mentioned in one of her letters that she liked Akana Jewelers because of its location."

"No wonder your room was the worst," Chloe

murmured, as all the pieces started to come together. "She was looking for those letters as well as the diamonds."

"All I know is that Nanette came back to the Whistling Duck empty-handed. I couldn't calm her down until I promised to call Chloe and ask her to meet us, so she'd give me back the diamonds."

"Then what happened?" Cade prodded.

"We went to bed. The next morning, Nanette went out to buy us breakfast and I went to the bathroom."

"And...?" Chloe prompted.

Gino's gaze dropped to the floor. "And I couldn't get out of the bathroom. The door had jammed somehow. Nanette told me goodbye, and I heard the door to our motel room close." He rubbed one hand over his face. "I was stuck in the bathroom overnight before I worked up the courage to jump out the window. Then I came straight here."

"Why here?" Cade asked.

"I thought Nanette might be here."

She couldn't believe it. "You told Nanette about our safe house? That's a Galetti family secret, Gino! How could you?"

Gino shrugged. "I wanted her to have someplace safe to hide if the heat got turned up. Besides, what is Cade doing here if it's such a big family secret?"

Chloe didn't have a good answer. "That's different."

"How?"

Because I love him. But she didn't say the words. Gino thought he was in love, too. Maybe they were both wrong. She was too confused to think clearly with Cade standing so close beside her. "It just is. Anyway, Nanette's not here."

"Then where is she?" Gino rose to his feet. "I need to find her. I'm worried about her."

Chloe reached for his hand. "The police are the ones who have to find her. And you should be worried about yourself. I just hope they don't charge you as an accessory."

He paled. "The police?"

"That's right, Gino," Cade said, his icy tone sending a chill through Chloe. "We're turning you in."

Cade squared his shoulders, preparing himself for a fight. But Gino didn't argue with him. He looked almost resigned, even relieved.

Chloe, however, was another matter.

"We?" she echoed, spinning around to face Cade. "Can't we at least discuss this first?"

"Okay, forget *we*," Cade said. "I mean *me*. Gino, let's go."

"I don't think I can walk," Gino said, wincing as he tried to put weight on his ankle. The effort made him lose his balance.

"That's all right," Cade said, grabbing him by one arm. "I can haul you out of here over my shoulder."

"No, I can do it." Gino wriggled out of his grasp, then limped toward the concrete steps.

Cade started after him, but Chloe grabbed his arm as Gino reached the stairs. "Let him go. He won't get far on that ankle."

"I have more questions for him," Cade said, his tone rough with frustration. "But he won't answer them, will he?"

"No." Her mouth thinned. "Because of Nanette."

Cade shook his head, feeling sorry for the poor sap. "She must be quite a number."

"I've never met her," Chloe told him. "She was my mother's cellmate for a few months last year. It was Mom's first and last attempt to play matchmaker."

"That's best left to the experts."

Chloe arched a brow. "Like Grandma Hattie?"

"Maybe." His gaze locked with hers and that familiar hunger gnawed away at his insides. She looked rumpled and distraught and utterly gorgeous. He could get used to looking at Chloe Galetti across the breakfast table every morning. But he had no intention of looking at her through a bulletproof partition in a prison visitor's room. "Unfortunately, I'm a wanted man at the moment."

"In more ways than one," she murmured, turning to follow Gino up the concrete steps.

Chloe sat in the back seat of her car, trying to talk some sense into her brother. An arduous, if not impossible task. To her surprise, Cade hadn't said a word from the driver's seat for the last twenty minutes. Unfortunately, neither had Gino.

She'd been carrying on a one-way conversation with her brother for the entire trip, trying to convince him that Nanette was trouble, not his true love. She wasn't even sure he heard her. Gino sat in mute silence, his eyes bright with the glow of martyrdom.

The car slowed to a stop, then Cade cut the engine. Chloe looked out the window, surprised to see her house looming before them. "What are we doing here? I thought we were headed for the police station."

"Your brother will have the best chance to make a deal if he cooperates fully with the authorities," Cade replied. "I thought if he brought Nanette's letters with him to the station as documented evidence of her involvement, he might score some points."

"I don't want to score points," Gino said, finally breaking his silence. "I want to take the rap for the woman I love."

Chloe swallowed a groan. She should have known. One of Gino's favorite stories as a child had been about their Great-Uncle Teddy. He'd lived on the right side of the law, sliding his toe over the line only a few times. Then he'd met a woman who called herself Rose Thorn, con artist extraordinaire. She had more scams than scruples, but after more than a decade of criminal activity she finally got caught. Then Great-Uncle Teddy stepped in to take the rap for her. It was the Galetti family's greatest tragic romance. Also, its greatest irony. The Galetti who had served the longest prison sentence was also the only one who had never committed a crime.

Panic welled up inside of her. "Gino, you can't..."

Gino's excited exclamation cut off his sister in midsentence. "Nanette's here!" He popped the car door open, then bounded to the front porch, where a blond bombshell wound her arms around his neck and gave him a torrid kiss.

"Well, this isn't good," Cade said from the front seat.

"We have to do something," she said, watching in bemused amazement as the kiss went on... and on... and on.

Cade opened the driver's door. "Okay, you take your brother, I'll take the blonde."

Chloe joined him out on the street. "Forget it, cowboy. That woman has a killer body and she's not afraid to use it. You wouldn't stand a chance. I'll take the blonde; you take my brother."

"Give me some credit." He followed her up the sidewalk. "I can resist a killer body."

She shot him a skeptical glance over her shoulder. "Remember the first night we met? You almost went into a coma when you saw me."

"In my defense, I was medicated at the time. You know my toe situation."

She bit back a smile. "Yes, I'm well aware of it. Let's just say you didn't seem to be feeling any pain. Or maybe that was due to the pretty blonde that was leaving Elk Creek Ranch as I pulled in."

"I'm not partial to blondes anymore." He gave her a long, lingering look. "Brunettes are more my style now. And in case you didn't know it, Chloe, you happen to be pretty spectacular."

Her cheeks warmed. "Thanks, but I'm still taking the blonde."

By the time they reached the front porch, the

young lovers had disappeared inside. Chloe turned to Cade. "Okay, now what's our plan?"

"Simple. We'll round 'em up and take them both to the police station." He stepped up to the door, leaning over to give her a swift, sweet kiss. "Then we continue what we started this morning."

He opened the door before she had a chance to disagree. Or agree. Or say anything. He was making unilateral decisions again, but at this point she rather liked his take-charge attitude. Cade made it all sound so easy.

Then she saw what lay beyond the door and knew it wouldn't be easy at all.

Cade stared at the blond woman standing in front of him. But it wasn't her body that held his attention.

It was the .38 Special in her hand. The one pointed straight at his chest.

He shifted in front of Chloe to shield her from the barrel of the gun. "You must be Nanette."

"Don't move a muscle, big guy," Nanette told him. Cool deliberation shone in her hazel eyes. One look told Cade she was devoid of both passion and compassion. Nanette wasn't the warm, affectionate woman Gino had described. She was as cold as ice and looked much too comfortable with a gun in her hand.

"We want the diamonds," Nanette said. "Don't we, Gino?"

Gino stood behind her, his Adam's apple bobbing in his throat and his face pasty white. "You promised no guns, sweetheart. Remember?"

"Don't wimp out on me now, Gino. We've come too far to leave here empty-handed."

"Forget the diamonds," Gino implored her. "We've still got each other."

Nanette laughed. "You've always been able to crack me up." She waved the gun toward Chloe. "Is that your sister?"

Gino cleared his throat, then made the introductions. "Nanette, this is my sister, Chloe. Chloe, this is Nanette Twigg."

Nanette dismissed Chloe with a disdainful glance, then slid her wintry gaze over Cade. It made his blood run cold.

"Not bad," Nanette said appreciatively, her gaze moving up and down Cade's body. "Your sister has good taste." A smile creased her lips. "Must run in the family."

"Thanks, sweetheart," Gino murmured, his cheeks flushed with love. Then he looked up at his sister. "Isn't she something?"

"Your girlfriend is holding us at gunpoint," Chloe told him.

"I'm his fiancée," Nanette informed her. "The engagement is back on."

Gino turned toward his sister. "Don't worry, she won't hurt you. We're leaving today for Mexico. It's so beautiful there—a great place for a honeymoon. I've got some travel brochures up in my room if you want to see them."

"Gino," Nanette said between clenched teeth, "shut your mouth. We can't tell them where we're going. We can't tell anybody."

"Now hold on, Nanette," Cade said, his gaze trained on the gun, "is that any way to talk to your fiancé?"

"I'll talk to him any way I want," Nanette retorted.

Gino's brow furrowed. "Are you saying my own sister can't come to the wedding?"

"Some sister," Nanette said with a snort. "You told me she's ready to turn you over to the cops."

Gino pointed to Cade. "It was his idea. I was going to take the rap for you, baby."

"There's no need for you to do that now," Nanette said with a smile. "This delicious cowboy will take the rap for both of us."

Chloe sucked in her breath. "What's that supposed to mean?"

"It means your brother's been worried about you, Chloe." Nanette said. "He doesn't like you hanging around such a loser. So, I've taken care of his little problem and my little problem all at the same time."

Chloe's fingers curled lightly around Cade's biceps. "I still don't understand."

Cade fixed his gaze on Nanette. *That's right, Chloe, keep her talking. Distract her.*

"It means your boyfriend is going down for the jewel heist." Malicious amusement gleamed in Nanette's eyes. "The cops are already looking for him. It should just be a matter of time before they collar him and bring him in."

"But they don't have any evidence against Cade," Chloe said.

"Don't you read the newspapers? The cops found a stolen ruby in his truck. That sounds pretty incriminating if you ask me."

Gino tapped his fiancée on the shoulder. "Uh... Nanette, I never really agreed to anything like that."

"I did it for you, darling," Nanette replied, neither her attention nor her gun hand ever wavering. "You want this cowboy out of your sister's life, don't you?"

"Well, yeah, but..."

"With Cade Holden behind bars, you don't have

to worry about your sister, and I don't have to worry about the cops tailing us. We can start our marriage off right."

Gino looked from his sister to his fiancée and back again. "I've got to think about this for a minute."

"There's nothing to think about," Nanette said sharply. "It's already done. I even went back to the jewelry store and dropped Holden's wallet in the bushes for good measure. That will place him at the scene of the crime. And didn't you tell me he has a police record?"

Gino nodded, looking completely bewildered now. "Yeah. So?"

"That means they'll nail him good. He'll be in prison forever." She smiled. "And we'll be someplace else, living happily ever after."

"You're forgetting one thing," Cade said, wanting to rattle her.

Nanette arched a penciled brow. "What's that?"

"You don't have the diamonds."

Chloe's hand tightened on his arm as an angry flush mottled Nanette's cheeks. "Cade, don't..." she whispered.

Nanette took a step closer to them, the gun steady in her hand. "Give them to me. Now."

"Gee, I'd love to," Cade said, "but I don't have them on me."

Nanette cocked the gun. "I'm counting to three, Holden..."

"Forget it." Chloe stepped in front of Cade. "You can't have the diamonds and you can't have my brother. I'd rather see Gino behind bars than trapped for the rest of his life with someone like you."

Cade yanked Chloe back behind him, his heart pounding hard in his chest. For the longest seconds of his life, the gun had been aimed straight at her chest. If he'd been uncertain about his feelings before, he wasn't now. He was absolutely furious with her. And almost beside himself with fear and love.

"Stop moving!" Nanette screeched, jerking the gun between them.

"All right," Cade said in a low, soothing voice. "We won't move anymore. You're all right. You're fine."

"I'm not fine! I want my diamonds." She held the gun higher. "I may have missed at the Dairy Wizard, but I guarantee you I won't miss at this range."

Gino turned on Nanette, his eyes wide. "You mean it's true? You shot at my sister?"

"Yes, after I planted that ruby in Cade's pickup truck, I decided to have some fun," Nanette replied. "I just wanted to scare her."

"It worked," Chloe muttered.

"Scare her?" A muscle knotted Gino's jaw. "Why? She's never done anything to you."

Cade saw his chance. He might not be close enough to reach for the gun, but Gino was in the perfect position to grab it. "A man doesn't let anyone threaten his family," Cade told him, desperately hoping Gino would listen.

"Shut up," Nanette snarled.

Cade ignored her. "Can you really love a woman who would try to hurt your sister?"

"Nanette is the girl of my dreams," Gino muttered, closing his eyes. "But this is a nightmare."

"This is reality," Cade told him. "Sometimes our dreams can overtake our common sense. Make us want something that doesn't exist. Nanette doesn't really love you. She's using you." He took a deep breath, praying this worked. "Open your eyes, Gino. See for yourself."

Three heartbeats later, Gino finally opened his eyes. He looked at Nanette with the gun in her hand, her mouth pressed into a firm, determined line. Then he turned to see his sister, partially shielded behind Cade's body.

"I love you, Gino," Chloe whispered. "No matter what happens."

The confusion disappeared from Gino's eyes and determination took its place. He turned back to

Nanette, and for the first time, Cade saw the potential of the man in front of him.

Gino took a deep breath, then held out his hand. "Give me the gun."

"Are you crazy?" Nanette whipped her long blond hair over her shoulder. "Don't listen to him. He's just trying to trick you. I'm the only one you can trust. The only one who really loves you."

"It's over, Nan," Gino said gently, reaching for the gun.

She spun on him, her eyes wild with fury. "It's over for you, Gino!"

Then she shot him.

Chloe screamed as Gino grabbed his thigh, then crumpled onto the floor. Blood soaked through his faded blue jeans.

Nanette whirled back around to face Cade and Chloe. "Now maybe you two will quit fooling around. I want those diamonds and I want them right now!"

She practically screamed the last words and Cade knew she was on the edge of losing control. Gino lay behind her, still clutching his leg. Then he looked up and made eye contact with Cade.

At that moment, Cade knew exactly what Gino was thinking. That probably should have scared him, but he didn't take the time to consider the implications. Instead, he nodded imperceptibly at Gino, then cleared his throat to get Nanette's full attention. "All right. We'll give you the diamonds."

Nanette's thin shoulders relaxed a fraction. "Finally. Where are they?"

"Right in plain sight," he improvised, watching Gino out of the corner of his eye. "We hid them in the chandeliers."

In the same moment Nanette looked up at the ceiling, Gino rolled toward her ankles, flipping her backward over his prostrate body. She hit the floor hard, a shot ringing out harmlessly as the impact knocked the gun from her hand.

Cade dove for it while Chloe scrambled toward her brother. He reached the gun just as Nanette got back on her feet. "Hold it right there," Cade ordered, rising to his feet to face her, his back to the front door.

"No!" Nanette screamed, her face twisted with anger. "This can't be happening!" But she didn't move.

"Cade," Chloe gasped, her face ashen as she cradled her unconscious brother in her arms. "I think he's dead."

"He's not dead," he reassured her gently. "He just fainted. He did the same thing after he dropped that power saw on my foot."

Nanette uttered a small cry, catching Cade's

attention once more. Her eyes widened and her mouth began to tremble as she worked up some hiccupping sobs. Big, crystal tears spilled over her cheeks as she held up her hands. "Please don't shoot me! I don't have your diamonds. I swear I don't. Please don't hurt me anymore."

Cade's brows furrowed at her bizarre words. Maybe the woman had finally gone over the edge. Then he felt a cool breeze on his back and glanced over his shoulder at the front door.

It was standing wide open.

And there was a police officer crouched in the doorway, his legs spread wide apart and his gun at the ready. "Drop your weapon," he ordered. "You're under arrest."

10

"Why won't you believe me?" Chloe sat in a tiny interview room at the Pine City Police Department. "Cade Holden did not steal those diamonds!"

Sergeant Clemens, a middle-aged woman with unsettling gray eyes, folded her hands on top of the table. "Ms. Galetti, even you have to admit your story is a bit far-fetched. Diamonds under the staircase? Assault by a Chihuahua?" The sergeant glanced down at her notepad. "And let's not forget shots fired at an abandoned Dairy Wizard."

"It's all true! Ask Cade if you don't believe me."

"I already have. And now I'd like to ask you a few more questions."

Chloe fought back an urge to scream. She'd been answering questions for the last two hours. At least the officer had assured her that Gino was out of danger and recovering at Sisters of Mercy Hospital. Unfortunately, he'd been heavily sedated and couldn't give a statement to the police. Not that the cops seemed overly eager to believe any Galetti. She just hoped Cade was having better luck.

After this fiasco, she'd be lucky if he ever wanted to see her again.

The sergeant flipped to a clean page in her notepad. "When you discovered the diamonds under the staircase, why didn't you contact the police?"

Chloe swallowed a sigh of impatience. She'd been over this story three times already. "I was afraid my brother might be... involved. I wanted to find him first and give him a chance to explain."

"And tampering with evidence didn't concern you or Mr. Holden?"

"No... I mean, yes. Of course, it did. Cade wanted to turn the diamonds over to the police immediately. But I convinced him to wait."

"Was this before or after you kissed him?"

Chloe blinked. "What?"

The sergeant consulted her notes. "According to Mr. Holden, you kissed him shortly after he discovered the diamonds under the staircase."

"That wasn't really a kiss." She hesitated. "I

thought he'd stopped breathing, so I was trying to give him mouth-to-mouth resuscitation."

"I see," the sergeant replied, scribbling more notes.

"No, I don't think you do." Chloe sat up straighter in the wooden chair. "Cade found the diamonds and got hit on the head. I thought he was dead and gave him mouth-to-mouth. Only I found out he wasn't dead. In fact, I found out he was a damn good kisser. But that doesn't have anything to do with what happened later."

Sergeant Clemens arched an inquisitive brow. "Anything else he's damn good at?"

Chloe frowned. "Nothing that's connected to this investigation."

"I'm just trying to establish the nature of your relationship."

She swallowed. "How did Cade describe it?"

"I prefer to ask the questions, Ms. Galetti. That way I can determine if your story matches that of the suspect."

"We're... friends." She hesitated. "Well, not really friends. We haven't known each other very long. The night we found the diamonds was only the second time we met." So much had happened since then it seemed like a month had passed instead of just a few days. "Actually, it was supposed to be a business meeting."

The sergeant's stubby pencil paused in midair. "But you just told me you kissed him."

"It's rather complicated," Chloe explained, wishing she'd kept her mouth shut.

"Why am I not surprised?" Sergeant Clemens sat forward in her chair. "But I'd still like to hear about it."

"It all started when I met Hattie Holden," Chloe began. Then she told her about Cowboy Confidential and Hattie's reputation as an amateur matchmaker. How Chloe had coerced Cade into rehiring her brother and everything that had happened since then. Well, almost everything.

"So, you see," Chloe said at last, "it's really all my fault. I'm the one who got Cade into this mess."

Sergeant Clemens stared thoughtfully at her. "I just have one more question, Ms. Galetti."

"What is it?" she asked wearily.

"Are you in love with Cade Holden?"

This time she didn't hesitate at all. "Yes."

Cade sat alone in his jail cell, wondering what was happening with Chloe. After the police had arrived at her house, they'd handcuffed Cade, called an ambulance for Gino, and retrieved the gun from the floor.

As he was led out of the house to a waiting police cruiser, he could hear Nanette shrieking about her innocence and accusing Cade and Chloe of not only stealing the diamonds but shooting Gino. Unfortunately, the cruiser pulled away before he saw either woman emerge from the house.

He looked around the jail cell, where he'd been sitting for more than two hours after his interview. The cell looked the same as it had during his outlaw days. The same uncomfortable bunks and depressing gray walls. The smell in the air was the same too—a musty mixture of sweat and desperation.

But he was a different man now.

They'd taken his cowboy hat at the processing desk, along with his other personal effects. But at least they hadn't made him change into one of those orange jumpsuits. To him, that meant he might have a chance of avoiding charges.

The faint sound of approaching footsteps made him rise off his bunk and walk over to the iron bars separating him from freedom. He just wanted to find Chloe and make sure she was safe.

The footsteps grew louder, then a familiar face rounded the corner.

"Oh, it's you," Cade said to his brother. "I was wondering if you'd drop by for a visit."

Nick wore his standard police detective clothes—black slacks and a blue button-down shirt with his badge pinned to the pocket. "Stop by?" he exclaimed. "What in the hell are you doing here, Cade? I couldn't believe it when I heard my little brother was locked up—again."

Cade held up one hand. "Hey, that's not fair."

"Fair?" Nick echoed, clearly furious. "What's not fair is that you've kept me in the dark about these stolen jewels and your involvement in this case. I've been texting you and calling your cell phone ever since I saw your name in that newspaper article."

Cade couldn't remember the last time he'd seen Nick this angry. "We dumped our phones after we saw the article. We couldn't chance the police tracking them to find us until we found Gino."

Nick clenched his jaw. "I'm so tempted to get the keys to this cell so I can come in there and kick your butt."

He'd never been afraid of a fight, but in that moment, Cade was glad there were iron bars between them. "You haven't even heard my side of the story."

"And I can't," Nick bit out. "Not now. As your brother, I can't be involved in your case. The only thing I could do was get you these nice accommodations all to yourself."

"I don't need any special favors."

"Too bad. It's for your own protection," Nick told him. "Usually, the guys in these cells don't feel too kindly toward cops or their kin." Then he lowered his voice. "Just tell me one thing. Should I be worried about you? Should Grandma Hattie be worried?"

Cade was tempted to tell him everything, but that wouldn't be fair to Nick. It was his brother's job to solve crimes in Pine City, and Cade didn't want to contribute to any divided loyalties that Nick might feel.

"I don't think so, but I can't be sure. The only thing I will say is that I didn't do anything illegal. Hopefully, I'll be out of here soon and I can tell you the whole story on our next visit to Wildcat Tavern."

"If there is a visit." Nick shook his head. "Damn it, Cade, do you realize how much trouble you're in because of Chloe Galetti? I still can't believe you got mixed up in all of this."

"You're one to talk," Cade scoffed. "As I recall, Lucy took you down some pretty dangerous paths before you two walked down the aisle together."

"That was completely different."

Cade walked over to his bunk and sat down.

"Thanks for stopping by, Nick. I'll see you when I get out of here."

"I sure hope so," Nick said, hesitating a moment. "I just have one more thing to say—get a lawyer." Then he moved away from the jail cell and headed back down the hallway.

An hour later, Cade was finally called back into a different interview room. This one was a small square room constructed with concrete blocks that had been painted a pale green. The only furniture was a rickety wooden table and matching chairs.

"Look, I admit it's all my fault," Cade began, determined to make that clear to Sergeant Clemens. He leaned back in his chair and watched as she methodically jotted a few lines in her notepad.

At last, the sergeant looked up at him. "Your fault? Have you decided to make a confession, Mr. Holden?"

He scowled. "No. I already told you Nanette Twigg is to blame for the robbery and the shooting and for locking Gino in that motel bathroom. She's also the one who clobbered me with the Chihuahua."

Sergeant Clemens nodded. "Ms. Twigg's story does have some inconsistencies."

"The woman is a consummate liar. Just look at how she conned Gino into thinking she was the girl of his dreams." He breathed a long sigh. "The poor guy actually thought he was in love."

"Maybe it was for real."

Cade shook his head. "Nanette doesn't respect him. She certainly doesn't care about him. She just wanted to use him to fulfill her own criminal fantasies. Love is about compromise. It's about sharing everything—dreams, hope, loss. But most of all, it's about wanting the very best for the one you love. And to do whatever is possible to make that happen."

She furrowed her brow "You sound like an expert in the matter."

"I certainly wasn't before I met Chloe Galetti." He took a deep breath. "But I'm working on it."

"Does that mean you're covering up for Ms. Galetti? Or are you two in this together?"

Before Cade could answer, the door opened, and a uniformed police officer stuck his head in. "Hey, Sarge, a call just came in from Akana Jewelers. It's the strangest thing. They just got all those stolen diamonds back in the mail. No return address."

"Just the diamonds?" Clemens asked him. "Not the other gems that were stolen?"

"Just the diamonds," the officer confirmed before leaving the interview room.

Sergeant Clemens turned back to Cade. "From

the information I've gathered, I'm starting to believe you were right about Ms. Twigg planting that ruby in your pickup truck. Especially since Ms. Twigg swore you all had the stolen jewels in your possession."

He breathed a sigh of relief. "Thank you believing me."

"Do you have any idea who mailed the diamonds back to the jewelry store?"

Cade hesitated. "Before I answer any more of your questions, I've been advised that I should ask for a lawyer."

The sergeant nodded. "Well, given the evidence we have so far, it looks like you may be off the hook, Mr. Holden. Especially now that the diamonds have been recovered." She jotted a few more notes down before rising out of her chair and heading for the door. Then she hesitated, finally turning back around to face him. "I understand your grandmother owns Cowboy Confidential."

"That's right," he said, confused by the sudden change of topic.

Sergeant Clemens cleared her throat. "I'm recently divorced, and it's been hell trying to meet decent, single men my age. Do you really believe Hattie Holden can help me find my perfect match?"

"Yes," Cade said with all the conviction of a true convert. "I do."

11

Two weeks later, Chloe sat nervously in her chair, waiting for the parole hearing to begin. She'd driven to the North Texas Women's Correctional Center just after lunch, leaving Gino in the care of the counselors at the innovative Craig Clinic, where Hank Holden's wife, Dr. Rachel Grant Holden, was a psychologist and managing partner.

Gino was in recovery from both his gunshot wound and his emotional issues. Chloe could already see a change in him, a maturity that she'd never glimpsed before. Maybe because she'd always treated him as if he were still a little boy.

The police had agreed not to press any charges against Gino in exchange for him turning state's evidence against Nanette. Surprisingly, it had been Gino's idea to seek counseling. For the first time, she had hope that her brother might finally be able to lead a happy life.

More hope than she had for herself.

She'd only seen Cade briefly after they were released from police custody, and then he'd been in the company of Sergeant Clemens. He'd looked so tired, with the heavy shadow of beard stubble on his cheeks and dark circles under his eyes. And yet she'd barely been able to keep from throwing her arms around him.

Chloe wished now that she'd given in to her impulse, since it was the last time she'd seen him. She knew he was working overtime to complete the work on Carly's Café, but whenever she showed up at the café to check on the painters or deliver the custom-made tablecloths, he'd conveniently disappear. It was obvious he was avoiding her.

And it was her own fault for involving him in Galetti family business.

She and Cade had spoken on the phone a few times, when Chloe had called him about small changes to her design plans for the café. Their conversations had been stilted and filled with long, awkward silences. In truth, she could have just communicated with him by text message, but she kept longing to hear his deep voice. Absence had certainly made her heart grow fonder, although she'd bet that Cade was reveling in his Galetti-free days.

And could she blame him? He'd overcome his outlaw past until he'd met her. Every newspaper article about the apprehension of the jewel thief, Nanette Twigg, had included information about Cade's police record, as well as the shooting of Twigg's paramour, Gino Galetti. The story had created quite the sensation in the sleepy town of Pine City.

The uproar was finally dying down, but she could only imagine what Cade's brothers and Hattie Holden thought of her now.

She pushed that thought out of her mind, wanting to focus on her mother today. The parole board meeting was being held in a conference room near the prison's front office. A nutmeg-brown carpet covered the floor and plastic molded chairs were set up in three neat rows, with a center aisle in between them.

A long conference table sat empty at the front of the room, close to an open doorway. The double doors at the back of the room were open too and a uniformed guard stood at the entrance as a few people shuffled inside. Most of them were Galettis. She saw her cousins Viper, Frankie, and Lenny seated together on the other side of the aisle. Ducky had taken a chair in the second row in front of her, along with Uncle Marco and Aunt Tina.

Chloe nibbled on her bottom lip, worried the Galetti family support might hurt her mother's chances for parole rather than help. But it was too late to do anything about that now.

A flurry of movement at the front of the room made her look up and she saw the three members of the parole board walk in. They seated themselves at the conference table, speaking quietly to each other as they arranged the notepads and water glasses in front of them.

Chloe twisted her fingers together as she studied them. There were two men and one woman who held the fate of her mother's freedom in their hands.

Eileen Galetti walked into the room, looking remarkably cool and poised for a woman teetering on the brink of freedom. Her hair was neatly drawn back in a matronly bun, making her look older than her fifty-two years, and she was accompanied by a female prison guard who led her to a chair in the front row. Once seated, Eileen turned around and smiled at Chloe, then gave a small wave to the rest of the Galetti family.

Chloe's gaze moved to the parole board members, who were observing her mother with keen interest. The head of the parole board was seated at the center of the table. He was an older man with a receding hairline, wearing a navy-blue suit and a pair of bifocals perched on the end of his nose.

He cleared his throat. "Good afternoon. It is now two o'clock, so we will begin our hearing in the matter of Eileen Maria Galetti. My name is Wesley Sullivan. To my right is Rochelle Evans, and seated on my left is Mateo Aguilar." Then he motioned to the guard. "Please close the doors to the conference room."

Chloe realized she was holding her breath and reminded herself to breathe. She swallowed hard as the social worker in charge of her mother's case walked to the front podium to give her report. For the most part, it was positive, although there was concern about Eileen Galetti's ability to secure employment, given her age and criminal record. The fact that her prior work experiences had been connected to her illegal activities didn't help much either.

"Well, that didn't go well," Chloe muttered to herself. She watched the social worker leave the room, then tried to read the faces of the parole board members. But all three of them were expressionless as they meticulously jotted notes down on folders in front of them.

After a few moments, the head of the parole

board shuffled through a few papers. "Is there anyone else present who wishes to be heard on this matter?"

"I do," Chloe called out. She stood up and walked to the podium, mentally rehearsing the speech she'd perfected over the last year—including her promise to provide housing for her mother and help her find a job. She only hoped they didn't ask for too many details. If her mother couldn't find a job, Chloe might be forced to sell the house and find something smaller just for the extra cash. But she didn't want to get ahead of herself. Hopefully, she could gloss over any potential obstacles and simply plead with the parole board to give Eileen Galetti one more chance.

Mr. Sullivan leaned forward. "Please state your name and your relationship to Mrs. Galetti."

"My name is Chloe Galetti and I'm her daughter."

He sat back in his chair. "Please proceed, Ms. Galetti."

She gripped the edge of the podium to steady herself. "I'm here to assure the board that I will do everything in my power to help my mother reestablish herself in society."

"Are you in a financial position to support Mrs. Galetti?" Ms. Evans asked.

"Yes, I've recently started my own business, so I'm optimistic about my financial future." Chloe suppressed a grimace, wishing she didn't sound so stilted. "And I'm determined to help her find full-time employment."

Ms. Evans raised a skeptical brow. "But will you have time to do so when you're also trying to get a business off the ground?"

"I will make the time," Chloe promised. "I'll do whatever I have to do."

Mr. Aquilar studied the notepad in front of him. "I see in my notes that Mrs. Galetti owns a house with you. Is that correct?"

"Yes, we own it together, along with my brother."

"So, housing for Mrs. Galetti won't be a problem?"

"Not at all," she assured him. The man was so stoic that she couldn't tell which way he was leaning.

Mr. Aguilar's brow furrowed. "About your brother...

But he was interrupted when the double doors to the conference room burst open and Hattie Holden strode into the room.

Chloe blinked. What was Cade's grandmother doing here? Then her heart skipped a beat when she saw Cade following in her wake. The steel-gray Western suit he wore emphasized his broad shoulders, and his sapphire-blue tie matched the color of his eyes.

Damn, he was gorgeous.

Cade met her gaze and her breathing hitched. Her hand tightened on the podium while her mind raced to find an explanation for his sudden appearance. She refused to believe the worst—that he'd come to wreak his revenge by sabotaging her mother's parole hearing. Still, he'd never expressed his outrage at everything that had happened to him, including the fact that he'd become a suspect in the burglary and been taken into custody.

And what about his grandmother? Hattie Holden couldn't be too happy about it, either. Although it was hard to tell by her expression. At the moment, the older woman just looked very determined.

Chloe watched Hattie parade right past her to stand in front of the parole board, her blue lace cardigan duster fluttering behind her.

"I hope I'm not too late," Hattie said, a little breathless.

Wesley Sullivan's brows rose at the sight of her. "Well, hello there, Mrs. Holden. I'm surprised to see you here."

Ms. Evans leaned toward him and said in a loud whisper, "Her grandson was falsely accused in a recent burglary involving the son of Eileen Galetti."

"Oh, of course." Mr. Sullivan nodded. "Are you here to make a statement?"

"I certainly am," Hattie said.

Chloe was aware that Cade had taken a seat across the aisle from her. From the way her neck burned, she knew he was watching her.

"As some of you know," she began, "I am Hattie Holden, the founder of Cowboy Confidential." Then she winked at the head of the parole board. "It's nice to see you again, Wesley. How is your new bride?"

Mr. Sullivan emitted a nervous cough. "She's fine. Wonderful, in fact. It's nice to see you again too. Are you personally acquainted with Mrs. Galetti?"

"We briefly met a few months ago and had a very nice conversation. However, both her son and daughter have recently been in my employ. I know you're fond of the Armadillo Coffeehouse, Wesley. Gino Galetti used to work there as a barista."

"Oh, him." Mr. Sullivan shifted uncomfortably in his chair. "Yes, he spilled a cup of cappuccino on me."

Hattie beamed. "Yes, that's him. You've probably seen his name in the newspapers recently."

Chloe swallowed a groan. This was not helping. But how could she stop her? Especially when it appeared that Hattie Holden and the head of the parole board were on friendly terms.

"Yes." Mr. Sullivan pulled a small stack of newspaper clippings from his file. "I have some of the articles right here. They say Gino Galetti was a person of interest regarding the burglary at Akana Jewelers."

"That's right," Hattie chimed. "His sister, Chloe Galetti, was tangled up in it, too, but the newspapers barely mentioned her at all."

Chloe closed her eyes, wishing she could sink right through the floor.

Mr. Sullivan set down the clippings. "The Galettis certainly are an... active family."

Mateo Aguilar leaned forward in his chair. "Didn't we just hold a hearing for a Kit Galetti last week?"

Mr. Sullivan nodded. "Yes, I believe she's a niece of Eileen Galetti. She's the one who called us pathetic morons after we denied her parole."

"That's right," said Rochelle Evans, scowling at Eileen. "I certainly do remember her."

Chloe's heart sank at their words. Not only would her mother not get parole this time, but she'd be lucky if they didn't make a recommendation to extend her sentence. Hot tears burned in her eyes, but she blinked them back. She'd become too used to disappointment over the years to fall apart now.

Mr. Sullivan steepled his fingers under his double chin. "Naturally, we cannot allow our feelings for Kit Galetti to prejudice our decision regarding Eileen Galetti."

"Naturally," Hattie echoed. "And I'm sure the fact that I'm offering Mrs. Galetti a full-time job at

Cowboy Confidential will make your decision much easier."

"What kind of job?" Mr. Sullivan asked.

"One that fits her unique skills," Hattie replied. "The demand for temporary employees has risen in Pine City and the surrounding area. I also offer benefits for my full-time staff."

Chloe held her breath, almost unable to believe what she was hearing. Then she looked at Cade and saw him watching her with those incredible blue eyes. She swallowed hard and looked away.

Could it really be possible that Hattie and Cade were here to help her mother instead of keeping her in prison? Could one of her dreams finally be coming true? The rest of the meeting passed in a blur and by the time it was over, Chloe learned her mother's fate.

Eileen Galetti was coming home.

The announcement was greeted with loud applause and cries of joy by the Galetti family members. Chloe waved to her mother as she was led out of the room, knowing that soon she'd be able to hug her again. With her heart full of gratitude, she turned to look for Cade.

But he was already gone.

"Would you like some more blackberry cordial, dear?"

Chloe sat at Hattie Holden's kitchen table, eating her third chocolate chip cookie, and drinking her second glass of Hattie's homemade blackberry cordial. The setting sun shone through the kitchen window, the beams reflecting the china set displayed in an antique hutch. "No, thank you. It's wonderful, but I just came here to thank you again for helping my mother. It means so much to me."

"Well, I was happy to do it. I think Eileen has a lot of untapped potential." A twinkle gleamed in her blue eyes. "I can't wait to see what she can do."

Chloe was still a little afraid of what trouble her mother might get into on the outside, but Eileen had promised her that she wouldn't do anything to endanger her parole. Eileen Galetti might play fast and loose with the law, but she's always kept her word to her children. "You've done so much for all of us. I don't know how we can ever thank you."

"I should be thanking you," Hattie said, joining her at the table with a plateful of honey buns still warm from the oven. "Everyone who's gotten a sneak peek at Carly's Café has raved about your work there. In fact, I have three interior design jobs available through Cowboy Confidential if you're interested."

Chloe smiled. "Can you include another bottle of

your blackberry cordial as part of the employment package?"

"Of course!" Hattie laughed, clapping her hands together. "Oh, this makes me so happy. You'll receive two bottles for each job, by the way, so I hope you can find someone to share them with."

"I'm sure my mother and Gino will love the cordial as much as I do." Chloe reached for a honey bun, avoiding Hattie's curious gaze. Neither one of them had mentioned Cade this evening, and she wasn't sure how to bring him up without revealing her feelings for him. Especially to the woman who'd thought they were a perfect match.

Hattie reached over to pat her hand. "You're a sweet girl, Chloe. I'm so glad you're part of the Cowboy Confidential family."

"Me too." She took another bite of her honey bun, then rose to her feet. "I really should get going. Thank you again for everything."

The oven timer dinged. "That's what I call perfect timing. The last batch of honey buns is finally done." Hattie walked over to the stove and used an oven mitt to pull out the hot baking pan. "Would you mind doing me a small favor?"

"Anything," Chloe replied.

"Cade loves honey buns, so if I box some up, could you drop them at his place on your way out?"

"Oh, I'd be happy to." Chloe was half embarrassed, half relieved. And more than a little suspicious that Hattie was trying to throw them together again. Although, she questioned if Cade even wanted to see her. "Do you know if he's at home this evening?"

"I'm not sure," Hattie said with a small shrug. She walked over to the cupboard and retrieved a plastic storage container. "We've started calving, so if he's not at the house, you can just leave the honey buns on the front porch."

"Okay, I'll do that," Chloe said, deciding to pour herself one more glass of blackberry cordial while she waited for Hattie to finish packaging up the warm honey buns.

Fifteen minutes later, Chloe drove the half mile to Cade's house and turned into the long driveway on the west side of Elk Creek Ranch. She'd debated whether she should knock on his front door or just put the honey buns on the porch and leave without seeing him. Especially given the fact that Cade had left the parole hearing without saying one word to her.

But Lorenzo and Eileen Galetti hadn't raised a coward. She was going to track down Cade at his house or search for him in a cow pasture so she could properly thank him for attending her mother's parole hearing.

But as soon as she rounded the curve in the driveway, she spotted him, and her heart leapt into her throat.

Cade sat on a bench near a small pond, located only a short distance from his house. There were two mallard ducks swimming there and he was tossing chunks of bread into the water for them.

She slowed to a stop on the gravel driveway and watched him, her car idling.

Chloe's heart skipped in her chest as she switched off the engine and climbed out of her car, then made her way toward him. He sat there, watching her and not saying a word.

"Hello," she called out.

"Hey there." He rose off the bench and walked over to meet her. "What are you doing here?"

Chloe handed him the storage container, still slightly warm to the touch. "I was just over at Hattie's place, and she asked me to drop off these honey buns for you."

One half of his mouth tipped up in a smile. "Oh, did she now?"

"I guess the woman never gives up," Chloe said. A strange thrill passed through her when she realized that Cade didn't look unhappy to see her. Just the opposite, in fact.

He nodded. "The Holdens are a stubborn bunch."

Chloe drank in the sight of him, wondering why he had this effect on her. The silence stretched between them. "Nice ducks," she said at last, pointing to the pond.

"Thanks." He turned toward the pond. "They just showed up one day and never left."

"It's such a peaceful place."

Cade tipped up his cowboy hat. "Grandpa Henry always told us boys to find a good thinkin' spot. Well, that bench by the pond is mine. I like to sit there whenever I have a problem to work out."

"I'm sorry I interrupted you."

He turned back to her. "I'm not. Maybe you can help me figure out my latest problem."

She smiled. "I'm happy to give it a try."

"Well, there's this woman I just can't get out of my mind. She's beautiful, kind, and talented. She drives me crazy, but in a good way." He reached out to gently brush a tendril of hair off her cheek. "So, I came out here to my thinkin' spot, but all I've been able to think about is spending all my days and nights with her." He took a deep breath. "The truth is, I love you, Chloe Galetti."

She was so stunned by his words she couldn't

speak. Her mouth was working but no words would come out.

Cade stared at her. He obviously took her silence as uncertainty because his expression grew more serious. "I know I'm not perfect by any stretch of the imagination. I can tend to be a little... stubborn."

His attempt at humility made her laugh. "A little?" she teased, finally finding her voice.

"I believe you called me a thickheaded cowboy the first night we met." He chuckled. "And I'm not saying you're wrong. But the way I see it, we need each other."

Her heart skipped in her chest. "We do?"

"Absolutely." He reached for her hand, his broad fingers gently squeezing hers. "It's true we haven't known each other very long. But it's also true that I can't imagine my life without you. I just hope you'll give me a chance to sweep you off your feet. Or at least let me sweep for you—I'm pretty good with a broom, if I do say so myself.

"Oh, Cade," she said, laughter and love bubbling up inside her. "Be still my heart."

"I'm serious, Chloe." He gazed into her eyes. "I've forced myself to give you some space these past couple of weeks, even though it's been sheer torture. I knew you needed time to take care of Gino and get your mom settled in, and to finish your work on the café. And I've spent that time working on becoming a better man so I could be worthy of a woman like you."

"What if I like you just the way you are?" she asked softly.

"Then you can take me for better or worse, although I promise to keep working on the worse parts." His smile turned playful. "And there are some better parts you haven't even seen yet."

Chloe laughed, then gave him a slow, lingering once-over. "What exactly are you offering, cowboy?"

"Myself."

Cade reached for both of her hands and clasped them in his. "I've wasted too much time searching for the perfect woman instead of looking for the woman who is perfect for me."

She smiled up at him with all the love in her heart. "I guess you had to become an outlaw again to appreciate the daughter of outlaws."

"It was worth it." He pulled her closer. "I'd go on the run with you anytime, anywhere."

"How about we just stay put on Elk Creek Ranch," she said, gazing up at him, "and make law-abiding babies."

His blue eyes widened. "Are you proposing to me, Chloe Galetti?"

"I sure am, cowboy. What do you say?"

He let out a loud whoop and then swept her up in his arms. "I say I'm the luckiest man in Texas."

"Cade, put me down." She laughed as he spun them around in a circle. "I'm too heavy."

"You feel perfect to me." Then he kissed her.

It was a long, slow, deep kiss that she never wanted to end. A kiss that touched her very soul.

They were both breathless when it was over. Cade turned and carried her toward the house. "Seems like we're completely right for each other after all. Maybe we should set a wedding date before you change your mind."

"I'm not going to change my mind." Chloe promised him, relishing the sensation of his strong arms around her. "But I do have a proposition for you."

His eyes lit up. "I can't wait to hear it."

"I propose that we hide out together in your house until we hash out all the honeymoon details." Then she pulled off his cowboy hat and placed it on her head. "Do we have a deal?"

"Deal," Cade said, bounding up the front porch steps with the love of his life in his arms.

Dear Reader,

Readers are an author's lifeblood, and the stories couldn't happen without you. Thank you so much for reading. If you enjoyed *Cowboy Outlaw* we would so appreciate a review. You have no idea how much it means to us.

If you'd like to keep up with our latest releases, you can sign up for Lori's newsletter @ https://loriwilde.com/subscribe/

To check out our other books, you can visit us on the web @ www.loriwilde.com.

Much love and light to you!

—Lori & Kristin

ABOUT THE AUTHORS

Kristin Eckhardt is the author of 49 novels with over two million copies sold worldwide. She is a two-time RITA award winner who loves writing romantic fiction. Her debut novel was made into a television movie called Recipe for Revenge. After earning a degree in Animal Science, Kristin and her husband raised three children on a farm on the Nebraska prairie. Along with writing, she enjoys baking, sewing, and spending time with family and friends.

Lori Wilde is the *New York Times, USA Today* and *Publishers' Weekly* bestselling author of 97 works of fiction. She's a three time Romance Writers' of America RITA finalist and has four times been nominated for Romantic Times Readers' Choice Award. She has won numerous other awards as well.

Her books have been translated into 26 languages, with more than four million copies of her books sold worldwide.

Her *Wedding Veil Wishes* series has inspired three movies from Hallmark that broke viewing records.

Lori is a registered nurse with a BSN from Texas Christian University. She holds a certificate in forensics, and is also a certified yoga instructor.

A fifth generation Texan, Lori lives with her husband, Bill, in the Cutting Horse Capital of the World.

COWBOY CONFIDENTIAL

Cowboy Cop

Cowboy Protector

Cowboy Bounty Hunter

Cowboy Bodyguard

Cowboy Outlaw

Made in the USA
Columbia, SC
17 August 2022

65522050R00141